HORSE AND CART
Stories from the Country

ELISABETH STEVENS

THE WINEBERRY PRESS

The author wishes to thank the following publications which have accepted several of the stories in this collection:

The Maryland Poetry Review — "The Dark-Eyed Boy"
Farmer's Market — "The Other People"
Late Knocking — "The Kill"

ISBN Number: 0-9612158-5-2
Library of Congress Catalog Card Number: 90-70945

Cover and illustrations designed by the author
Photograph by Laura Schleussner
Editor/Publisher: Elisavietta Ritchie
Typesetting and book design by Bruce Sager
   The TypeWorks, Hanover, Maryland

Manufactured in the United States
First Edition

The publication of this book has been made possible in part by The Mayor's Committee on Art and Culture (MACAC), Baltimore. Several of the stories were completed at The Virginia Center for the Creative Arts and at The Ragdale Foundation.

THE WINEBERRY PRESS
3207 Macomb Street NW · Washington, D.C. 20008-3327

"The undiscover'd country . . ."
Hamlet, William Shakespeare

HORSE AND CART
Stories from the Country

Table of Contents

To Josephine Jacobsen

The Dark-Eyed Boy

At the lake, the end of August . . . .

Morning sun expanding over pine-shrouded hills on the other shore, warming the red and green roofs of occasional cottages . . . .

Dark against light. Dark against light.

The lake is broken, broken, broken into blue-white sun ripples, black-green shadow troughs. At the north end of the lake in the long, empty marshes, the water is always dark. That's where the wilderness begins . . . .

Alone on the boat house dock after breakfast, I rest in one of the ancient Adirondack chairs by the swim ladder, half watching brown ducks swimming among yellow water lilies, half tasting maple syrup in the back of my mouth, and not doing anything else but breathing. I'm expecting. It's nine o'clock in the morning, but I'm almost asleep.

My husband, Dave, is taking the bags out of the cottage and packing them in the car. He does everything for me these days. We're checking out, heading home. He starts teaching Monday. I'm not teaching this year — I'm due in October. If it's a boy, he'll be David. If it's a girl, she'll be Rhea. That's my name.

Pursued or pursuing, two black birds soar screeching from the high pines and out over the moored motor boats in front of the dining hall. A dark feather falls to dark water. Ducks join the clamor. The small flock — a green-necked male, a small dark brown female and a larger light-brown female followed by her four fledglings — swim quacking to deep water.

Then, pounding down the dock from the cottage path, the boys arrive. Two of them, maybe ten, maybe eleven years old. I've seen them in the dining room. Not brothers. They sit at different tables. Their families come back every year. So do we.

The first boy is pale and pudgy. His hair is sun-bleached, almost white. The second is dark and sallow. Against the sun he seems as angular as a crooked stick. The boys are going to fish. They have brought their rods. They are going to fish right in front of me by the swim ladder. They are baiting their hooks. Maybe they know how to cast without hitting somebody behind them. Maybe they don't. I don't know about kids their age. I teach kindergarten.

I'm wearing a sepia-colored smock to look smaller — but I'm big. They can't miss me. Besides, my hair is red as fire with gold in it. It's long, and the breeze lifts it up to curl around me. They see me — I catch the dark eye of the sallow one as he turns to cast — but they pretend they don't. Their white lines sing, their silver hooks whirl.

Who wants to be a poor fish? I don't like to think about a

hook in an eye, an ear, or some place else soft.

I shift my weight. It isn't easy to get out of a deep-seated Adirondack chair in a hurry, but I do it. I head up the dock to the boathouse porch. My brown and red reflection floats among the water lilies where the ducks have taken refuge. Once, long before I was born, a woman by the name of Brown drowned down the lake. People still talk about it. There is an old man living who helped get her body out with grappling hooks. When it happened, he was just a boy. She was pregnant.

On the porch, I sit in one of the old rockers made of twisted branches. All summer, my feet have been swollen. I rest them on the log railing. The boys aren't catching anything. I could have told them. The lake was fished out even when I was little. Maybe they'll go now. But they don't. Instead, the dark-eyed boy develops another game.

The game, which brings them closer to me, is to cast into the shallows where the ducks are now swimming among the water lilies.

"Come on," he calls to his pale companion. "Come on." They cast. A shout. A fluttering of wings. Has a duck been hit? I can't see. An old couple, strolling down from the dining hall, is crossing in front of me, blocking my view. They nod, then amble on to settle in rockers beyond the doors to the racks for canoes and guideboats.

The ducks have scattered. The boys have dropped their rods. They are kneeling above the water lilies, peering under the dock.

"Is she there?" the dark-eyed boy demands.

"I don't see her," the pale one answers.

I notice that the little dark female, the fledglings and the green-necked male are swimming out beyond the dock again in the safety of deep water. One duck is missing.

The boys are standing up. They take their rods in their hands.

"Oh," the old woman says, "I hope they're not going to hurt the poor duck."

Just then, the lone, light brown female emerges from under the dock and drifts like a dry leaf towards the shallows of the rocky shore.

"There she is," exclaims the dark-eyed one. He raises his rod, then hesitates. The old woman is watching. Instead of casting, he lets the rod hang limply, hook in the water.

"Now I wouldn't want to hurt a duck with my hook," he announces loudly, as if to no one in particular. "But if my hook just happened to hit a duck in a hard part — like the beak — it wouldn't hurt."

The old man stands up. He is going to say something. The boy is lying. I can imagine the boys bending forward, flailing the duck with their rods, breaking her back, poking her under to drown.

Instead of speaking, the old man takes out his pipe and lights it. The woman is silent too. They exchange glances. I see what it is. They don't want to get involved.

The mother duck is standing in the sandy shallows. Her neck is twisted, her head is thrust back unnaturally.

"Oh look," the dark-eyed boy says, as if just noticing, "that duck by the rock has something wrong with her." He glances at his companion, then back at us. We are all watching. "See," he gestures to his audience, "she can't breathe through her nose any more, she has to breathe through her mouth." His eyes glisten. He is smiling.

The duck is poised in the shadow of a grey rock. Her beak is spread painfully wide. A frail, strangled hissing sound issues from somewhere deep within her throat.

The old man nods toward the path. "Let's go back to the

cottage," he says. I remember which one they have. It's the one called "Contentment" — I've seen them sitting on the front porch.

The old woman gets up. As they cross in front of me again, she glances back at the boy, who is standing facing us, legs astride, his friend behind him.

The old man relights his pipe as they start up the path. He blows out the match. The smoke lingers.

I am alone with the boys. The dark one gives me a look. Our eyes meet, he turns his back on me. He thinks I won't interfere — because of the baby.

The boys come nearer. They are poised beneath the porch at the dock's edge. Their shadows extend across the ripples to the shallows where the duck is. They raise their rods.

Because my hair is red, I get red when I get angry. My kids at school know. They stay out of my way.

"Stop!" I stand up, stick out my arm like a traffic cop, palm vertical. The sun from across the lake crosses my palm. It's hot — as if I were holding the light in my hand.

The boys have turned around. They are looking at me. The dark-eyed boy drops his rod. How small he is, how thin and frail. The pale boy drops his rod too.

The first boy turns his back to me. He is looking far away, way up the lake. "I don't care about that old bitch of a duck," I hear him say softly, as if talking to himself.

The game is over. I sit down.

"You bring the rods," the dark-eyed boy directs his companion. Without a glance in my direction, he begins to run. His thin feet pound across the dock, up the path. The pale one follows. Even though he is carrying the rods, he catches up easily.

Before they are lost behind the pines, the dark one lags, the pale one leads. At a distance, there is something odd in the laggard's silhouette. Is one shoulder higher? Is he hip-shot, crook-backed? No, it is something else, something I can't determine. The boys have disappeared. The black birds are screeching again.

I am alone on the dock.

Where is the mother duck? Has she hidden herself somehow? She is not in the shallows besides the shore. She is not swimming among the water lilies. She has not joined the flock out beyond the dock. The water is full of ripples. Is she under the water, lying at the bottom, drowned?

My throat is dry. I am very thirsty. The breakfast pancakes are heavy inside me. I cough, I gasp. I have to open my mouth to breathe. I open it wide. I need a glass of water. I'll have to go back to the dining hall to get one.

Afterwards, I decide to take the sandy road behind the cabins and find Dave. I could go back to the dock to wait for him, but I don't want to. Paddle-footed and slow because of my swollen feet, I pass behind several cottages, glancing between them at the lake beyond.

As I come to the one called "Prudence" — our cottage is only two beyond — I see a dark-haired woman standing on the porch.

"Come on," she calls to someone I can't see, "come and take your medicine."

"I don't want to." The answer comes from the far side of the cottage. It is a voice I recognize.

"You have to — " The woman's voice is tired, nasal. Perhaps she has said the same things many times. With an uneven gait, the dark-eyed boy emerges from the pines. Carrying his rod, he lopes across the front path. At the water's edge, he stops. The sun is in front of him.

Then, walking as slowly as he dares, he approaches the

woman who has to be his mother. She, seeing that he has given in, turns and goes inside. It isn't until he starts up the stone steps to the porch that he sees me. When he does, the look he gives me is like lightning. Then, taking his rod in both hands, he flails it with all his puny force against the wide boards of the porch.

Does the rod break? I don't wait to find out. Just the thwack is enough. Plodding on, I go along in back of the cottage as fast as I can — and almost step in it. Someone has vomited in the ferns under the pines.

Fresh, yellow, lumpy, redolent, it steams and gleams in the sunlight. Soundlessly, it is slipping from pale green leaves to the pine needles below.

I have an ache somewhere. Maybe it's my feet. I return to the soft, sandy road. Down beside the high firs, I see Dave. He is roping the canoe to the top of the van. He waves. I wave back. I am almost there.

"Are you all right?" Dave ties the last knot. Then he slides open the door of the van for me and helps me into the front seat after a quick hug.

"I guess so." The throbbing in my feet extends up my legs to my thighs.

"Do you remember that boy with the dark eyes — the crooked one?" I ask as he gets in beside me.

"You mean the sick one."

"What's wrong with him?"

"It's one of those incurable things, hereditary. I heard somebody talking about it in the dining room. It's got a long name, it's called — "

Before Dave, the science teacher the students like best, can explain, I interrupt. "Is it fatal?"

"Well, not right away maybe — but he isn't going to live to grow up."

"Oh."

Dave starts the van. As we bump slowly down the sandy road, I close my eyes. If the dark-eyed boy has come out of his cottage, I won't see him.

Instead, on the inside of my eyelids, I see light, then shadow. Light. Then shadow.

What is final pain like? I wonder, clasping my hands under the bulge where the baby floats sleeping in the dark. I can imagine the duck dead, I can imagine the boy dead, but I can't imagine their pain.

Pain, I guess, is something you can't imagine. You have to feel it.

Once again, I am almost asleep . . . .

The
Other People

The name is George. The main thing that happened was that when we came down the mountain we weren't the same as when we went up. That was because of the other people.

Me and Lily — we're ten years married — we had determined to make a picnic. It was September, a middle-of-the-month weekend when we were sure the people who drive out to the mountains at Labor Day wouldn't be there. We never go up old Bull in summer. That's because the Bull Mountain picnic place will be full. There's only so many fireplaces at the top, and it's getting harder to find wood.

This time, we brought our own wood with us. Skeeter, our boy, he picked up some of it in the woods behind our place. Minnie, our girl, she helped. We got into the pickup around four, and before five-thirty we were there with our fire going in a good fireplace — one of the ones that isn't broken down.

We were alone. That's the way we wanted it. Skeeter and Minnie were playing something down the slope with a ball I give them. Me and Lily were resting back on our blanket, she with a soda and I with a beer. I was watching the fire dance up and musing down at the littler mountains that ring the old Bull, rising and joining like the links of a chain.

Then, when I was watching the coals go from yellow to orange and thinking about getting the steaks I'd told Lily to put in the bottom of the cooler, I heard them. It was a car on the road — the grinding down on stones that tires make. Lily heard it too. She didn't say nothing, but since I had her hand, I felt her fingers tense. We didn't move or anything. We just waited.

Sure enough, pretty soon we saw an old blue van winding its way up. There were people in it, but we couldn't see who. When the van gyred around the final portion, I saw that the license was an odd color. Out of state.

Maybe it wasn't needful, but I called Skeeter and Minnie to come back. They didn't mind coming. They were tired of ball playing. They were hungry. I told Skeeter he could get out the steaks and Minnie the plates. I stayed where I was with Lily.

Then we saw the van come straight up towards us. It was coughing, probably needed a valve job, but they made it. Now there's a place you're supposed to park at the end of the road. There's a sign that says so, but not everybody sees it.

Either they didn't see it or they didn't care, because the fellow who was driving came up where you're not supposed to — right to where the Bull flattens out at the top. The place he parked was down a ways but smack in front of us, spoiling some of the view. The blue the van was was an ugly color — and rusty too.

The engine heaved after the driver shut her off. The plugs

weren't good probably. All the doors opened except the ones at the back. One man, two women, a baby and a kid littler than any of ours got out. Five of them, four of us.

I wasn't going to not speak to them, but I wasn't about to arrange a welcome party neither. I didn't get up or nothing: I just raised up a little on my elbow and waved a hand. "Hi."

"Hi." The man said that. The women didn't speak. And the kid was quiet too. The man was skinny and brown-haired, built like a string bean and wearing a torn undershirt. Nothing special to him, but the dark-haired woman with the baby that stayed close to him, had to be his wife, she was different. She was a beauty in spite of her worn jeans, her soiled sneakers. It wasn't just that her hair was so black: it also was that her skin was so white beneath it. Looked like coal and lime, and neither seemed real. Both were though — she was too young for them not to be.

It was Lily who stood up first. She said something about getting our napkins and knives and forks. While the other people were opening the van in back and unloading, I stayed on the blanket. Maybe I was mad they'd had to come where we were, maybe I was just tired. I work in the auto parts store all week. Helping people. "Yes, sir," and "Certainly, ma'am." When Sunday comes, don't ask me for help.

While Lily and Skeeter and Minnie were getting together what Lily had fixed, I just took the cap off another beer and watched the other people. Their kid, maybe five, maybe four, could have been a boy or a girl. You couldn't tell right off because it was just wearing shorts and a shirt and the hair was cut short in a funny sort of way. With the baby — there was no doubt. She was wearing a pork pink sweater with a little frilly collar and embroidery down the arms. She was milk-skinned like her mother, but her hair hadn't come in yet — she was bald as a suckling.

"Daddy — " It was my little Minnie. She's six and has got my red hair and some freckles that go from one cheek to another, right across the bridge of her nose. "Daddy, Skeeter can't find the steaks and Mommy can't either."

Minnie ain't beautiful, but I love her. I was going to get up, I would have had to get up anyway. I hugged Minnie and the beat-up baby doll she'd brought along with her. "We'll find 'em."

We started to our picnic table, but on the way I couldn't help thinking: Why'd those people have to take the south fireplace, the nearest one to us? You see, there are four fireplaces at the Bull Mountain picnic place — five if you count the center one in which the stones have fallen off and nobody's fixed them. The four good fireplaces are arranged at something like points of the compass. Ours, at the west, is the best for watching sunsets.

You'd think, just out of common courtesy, that those people could have gone to the east place over the rise. Maybe the view isn't as good, but then both families could have had their space and not seen each other. Of course, I wouldn't blame no one with kids for not taking the north, even though it is the highest. There's big rocks up there, and behind them where you might not expect it, a drop off that goes down a long ways.

When we got to the picnic table I caught the worried look on Lily's face, but just then, the other fellow found reason to bother us. Needed to borrow matches. I had a half-used pack, and our fire was going, so I gave them to him. We don't smoke.

What I didn't like was the way he asked for it. "Would you be so pleased as to give us a light?" I think that was the way he put it — kind of odd and sniveling like. There was something not right about the way he talked too, kind of foreign maybe. I guess the thing I really didn't like was his eyes peering at me and blinking all the time. His eyes were the palest sort of watery blue. You see eyes like that sometimes with brown hair like his, but they don't seem to match. Such eyes — so transparent it seemed you could look right through them like windows into his head — can make a person uncomfortable.

When he'd gone, Lily gave me the bad news. "George, we forgot the steaks." I was glad she waited, because I wouldn't have wanted him to see the look on my face.

"That can't be," I said.

"It is," she said. She had everything spread out on the table, and the steaks weren't there.

I tried to think back. I remembered getting the steaks out of the bag from the supermarket where Lily works part-time as a checker. I remembered setting them on the table in the center of the kitchen, the old one with the white enamel top. I remembered the way the meat looked too — red and white and oozing blood beneath the shiny plastic. Some people can be vegetarians and be perfectly satisfied. I'm a meat eater. Lily is too. Because Lily works at the market, we get the best.

So we'd come to the Bull, but the steaks hadn't. I thought I'd asked her to put them in the cooler bottom where they'd keep best. Maybe I had, maybe I hadn't. Probably those steaks were still sitting on the table, getting warmer, softening in the midst of darkening blood.

For a minute, the four of us stood there, looking at what we had. There was a big loaf of bread, apples, coffee, cupcakes for the kids, potato salad and coleslaw, catsup, sodas, more beer. No meat — not even a package of bologna.

"There's eggs and bacon in the truck," Minnie piped up.

"Ssh — " I said, not wanting the other people to hear.

Minnie was right though, because on the way I'd said to

stop off. I'd decided I wanted a big breakfast for Monday —
start the week right.

"Well," I told the three of them, trying to make the best of
it, "eggs and bacon it is."

The other people, close as they were, had to have heard
me, and then the strangest thing in the world happened.
Without being sure of where it came from, we heard what had
to be a laugh but wasn't like one but was instead more like a
gurgle, or even a strange bit of a song.

Who was laughing at us? The four of us looked around at
the other people The man she called Julien and the beautiful
black-haired woman he called Rose were kneeling with their
backs to us stuffing paper and twigs in under their grate. Their
pink baby was asleep on a pink carrier on their table top, and
the other kid — had to be a boy after all — was relieving
himself around the side of their van.

Then, looking up to the north spot where the big grey
rocks were, we saw who it had to be. It was the other woman
that come with them, the one who was dressed funny in a
long, yellow dress that furled down almost to her ankles and
didn't have a belt. She was standing up tall as a statue, facing
us with her mouth wide open and her eyes glassy.

"What's wrong with her?" Lily whispered.

We all stared. Even Minnie and Skeeter were quiet, but the
woman didn't laugh again. Instead, she just stayed there as
though her feet were set in concrete. The only part of her that
moved in the soft, late afternoon breeze was her boobs. She
had big ones. They shook a little. Side to side. Up and down.
Maybe she knew she was doing it. Maybe she didn't. It was the
biggest pair I'd seen in a long time.

Finally Julien and his woman noticed. When he saw us
looking, his face got dark, but he didn't say nothing. He just
got up slow and quiet as if it was nothing particular and went

up to the rocks after her.

When he got there, all he did was stand below her, facing up. He was smaller, she was bigger. Then, mouthing out the words real slow, he said: "Come, Sister." Then he just reached up and got her hands, both of hers in one of his, and led her off the rocks like a lamb.

On the way down though, he stumbled on something. She got ahead of him then, but they didn't loose hands, and for the rest of the way it almost seemed she was leading him.

Afterwards — I guess he felt he had to say something — he half turned his head in our direction, not really looking our way. "Deaf and dumb," he said quickly. That was all.

"Oh." Lily said that. She was embarrassed, I think, because the kids were gawking. Lily's a good woman. She's kind.

Right off, she got the kids turned around — sent them down the road a little ways where there's a stream so they could wash their hands. She said she'd get the eggs and bacon. I gave her arm a little squeeze then — Lily's arms are nice and soft. She's no great looker, but she's the woman I love.

Then, without the steaks to grill, there was nothing for me to do. So I went back to the blanket and rested for a while, watching things and trying not to want the steaks. The deaf and dumb woman was sitting quiet at their picnic table. Julien had called her "Sister", and she had to be that. Maybe she didn't have the same empty eyes he did, but since he couldn't see much, from the look of it, and she couldn't hear or talk, they were a pair.

When the kids were on their way back from the stream, they got talking to the other people's boy. For a while the three of them stood at the front of the blue van. Skeeter, who's nine, was the biggest, then Minnie. Beside them, the other people's boy was puny. When the kids started picking up little rocks and tossing them down the mountain, that one could barely hoist a pebble.

They weren't having steaks or even hamburgers, I saw, watching the black-haired woman. What they had brought to eat was some peculiar wound up sausage — looked like a snake. They put the whole length of it in a big black pan they had. As soon as it began to cook, it began to smell.

Maybe I closed my eyes at that point. I was worn out — and hungry too. When I opened my eyes, Lily was standing in front of me.

"Problem," she said. "No frying pan."

I looked at her. We always cooked our steaks on the grills they had there. We weren't going to fry potatoes, we had pota-to salad. We had a coffeepot for afterwards, but that was all.

"What'll I do?" Lily asked.

I sat up. I had thought already of driving back to get the steaks and given up on it. Twenty-five miles each way. I surely wasn't going fifty miles for a *pan*.

I looked at her — then at the other fireplace where the sausage was steaming and spitting grease that sparked the fire. Our fire was still burning, but of course there was nothing cooking on it.

"We could boil eggs in the coffee pot," I said.

"And the bacon — ?"

Lily and I were both thinking the same thing. I knew we were going to have to borrow their pan when they finished with it. I wasn't going to let her have to do the asking. I got up.

Just then, Skeeter came back to us. There was a little bruise on his cheek, kind of triangular, and it was connected to a little wriggly line of blood going down to his neck.

"What hit you?" I asked.

"It was nothing, just a stone."

Skeeter wasn't one to tattle. I knew that.

Then Minnie came running up. "Skeeter got hit by a stone Armand threw."

"Armand is their boy?" Lily said.

Minnie nodded.

"Maybe it wasn't on purpose," Skeeter said.

"Maybe it was," I said.

Lily didn't say nothing. She just got a napkin and took Skeeter back down to the stream to wash off, giving the other people a wide berth. Minnie went with them.

There was something growing up in me, but I didn't take note of it. Armand was down there by their table, but he wasn't looking my way. He was giving that tender little baby something to play with, sweet as pie.

I poked the fire, added a log where it was needed. Then — there was nothing else to do — I opened up another beer and watched those two women. They were standing at their table, fixing something.

The wife was the beauty, no doubt, but it was all in her face. Her body was thin, her chest flat, her stomach rounded a little as though she needed to suck in her breath. It was the dumb one who was worth watching. Never mind her hair hung in long, pale tangles — or that she was blank-faced, giving the feeling there was something wrong but you didn't know what. That woman was built.

When Lily came back with the kids — she'd stuck a little bit of the napkin to Skeeter's cheek and washed away the blood — she put it to me. "Are you going to ask 'em for the pan? Or will we just go home?"

"I'll ask." I slipped up to the high rocks behind the north spot to take a leak first. As I zipped up, I caught a glimpse of the deaf and dumb one down the slope. I was nearly certain she couldn't see more than my head and shoulders, but she was staring at me. Nothing wrong with her eyes, I guess.

From there, I took the long way, circling over east and down so I came out below where those people were. I didn't take no notice of Armand when I got there — nor the plump baby neither. And I didn't go to the man I'd given the matches to, I went to the black-haired beauty, and I said: "We forgot our frying pan, ma'am. When you're done cooking with it, could we borrow yours?"

I came at the right time. She'd served up the snake glop they'd been cooking. Wrapping a napkin around the hot handle, she gave me the pan while the rest of them watched.

I said: "Thank you." That's all I said. I didn't smile. They didn't either, except for the sister. Maybe I did look laughable, the big black iron thing out in front of me. Anyway, the sister kept a silly grin on her face.

The problem, after I'd got the pan back to Lily and poured out all the grease I could, was trying to get rid of the smell. Lily wiped it out with paper towels, but the snake stink was something only hot water and soap suds could have cured.

When we'd done all we could, Lily put the bacon in. It was good to see something on our fire, even if it wasn't steak. In the meantime, Lily give us potato salad and coleslaw and mixed up the eggs to scramble. There was plenty of bread.

When the bacon had cooked, I put the eggs on. The kids were hungry, irritable. Then, just as I about had things ready for them, that little squirt Armand had to sneak up above our table and cause more trouble.

They had finished eating, I guess, and they must have given him candy wrapped in colored pieces of paper. What he was doing was eating it piece by piece and then winging the papers down at us from behind a rock. One sticky pellet hit Lily on the back of the neck and went down inside her blouse. She had a time getting it out.

When that happened, I told Lily: "You stir the eggs." So

she did.

In barely a second — I'm fast when I need to be — I was up there behind his rock. I didn't *do* anything. I was using his mother's pan, wasn't I? Instead, I just give him a look, a long one, the kind that doesn't need words. His mouth was purpley from the candy he had, and he flashed me a funny little clown smile before he ran. Would you believe it? As he turned, that ugly kid winged one more of those tinfoils he'd wadded into little bullet balls to where Lily was with the pan.

When I got back to Lily the eggs were cooked — more cooked than I like them, in fact, brownish in spots where they'd stuck to their pan. We ate. Four of us at the table, but we barely talked. We ate a lot of bread. We tried to get the rest down. Poor Minnie, she's game for six, she is. She forked those eggs into her mouth and held them there so her cheeks were puffed out, trying to get the courage to swallow and then doing it all at once so she nearly gagged herself.

The flavor of the bacon masked the snake taste, but the eggs were terrible. They weren't like eggs at all hardly, they were like their food — worms or whatever it was they'd had.

Skeeter ate what he had on his plate without talking about it. What he did say was: "I don't like those people, they — "

He didn't get to say the rest of it. His mother made him shush.

Then I bit down hard on something in my eggs. Damned if it wasn't one of that boy's tinfoils. It was like clamping on ice — sent a chill through my molar. You can bet I didn't like that. I wished I had a whole lump of tinfoil to stuff down his throat.

Anyway, we finished it all and had the cupcakes. It was time to return the pan. Lily wanted to be nice, I guess, so she wiped all that was left of the eggs out of it — and the fat of the bacon too. She did all she could. It was up to me to take the pan back.

The handle was still warm, but I didn't bother to shield it with a napkin. I can handle hot. With my middle finger hooked through the hole in the pan handle, making the heavy thing swing, I headed to where I was supposed to go, but there was nobody there.

How could the five of them, sitting not that far away, have just gone and vanished? Their plates were there, their cups, their forks, even the smell of what they'd eaten was there. Then I saw. They were winding down the side of old Bull, going for an after supper walk. All but one of them, for just then, I heard another one of those laughs.

It was soft this time, more like a whispery cackle or a giggly call. The sister. It had to be, and it was coming from the van.

They had parked the old wreck backed up into some bushes so you couldn't see inside. The back doors though, painted with one of those snow-on-the-mountain scenes people like, were standing open. With the frying pan still hanging from my finger, I went around by the bushes to have a look.

Preparatory to sunset, the sun had fallen to hang like an orange painted on the sky. That sun was opposite those spread wide doors, flowing to the shadows inside in a golden way. And in there was the sister, and when she saw me she stopped laughing.

She was sitting on the rusty metal floor of the empty van, and I knew then why she'd worn her skirt so long. She was sitting crosslegged, and she wasn't wearing pants. She had her skirts pulled all the way up for a pillow behind, and the sun, even though it couldn't reach to her face, was waving and dancing and licking on her bare crotch. The dark curls of her hair around the open slit looked wet, and her hand was draped on her thigh as if she'd had her finger in there.

If I hadn't had the frying pan hooked on my finger, I would

have dropped it. But I didn't, I just stood where I was with the warmth of the sun pushing at my back. When she saw me, the sister didn't move, she didn't gurgle. Instead, she looked at me. And I looked at her.

Then, sliding that hand to the middle — I thought sure she was going to cover herself up — she put the index finger on one side of the slit and the middle finger on the other, and spread herself wide as she could. Open to the quick.

There were a lot of things I should have done then. The things I did do weren't among them. First thing: I didn't drop the frying pan. Second thing: I peered around the sides of the doors with the speed of light. Her brother and his wife, I saw, were still down the hill in front of the van. Lily and the kids, I saw, were still up to the side by our table.

The sun was almost to the point of touching the top pines on the hill across, but it wasn't there yet when I leaped in, unzipped and went at it, frying pan and all. I never did get to see her boobs, but I had one hand on them while she gurgled in a different way from before. When I backed out of that van with the knees of my jeans rusty, the sun had only come down the littlest ways on the point of the topmost pine — and I still had the frying pan.

Wouldn't you know it? When I stopped by their table and set the frying pan there as I'd meant to do all along, that little Armand turned up out of somewhere. I was pretty sure he hadn't seen me hop out of the van backwards, but I didn't have total security. But what could I do about it? What was I going to say to him — thanks for the tinfoil?

Money is the root of all evil, and this time was no exception. Anyway, just to cover myself, I tossed him a half dollar I'd been saving in the bottom of my pocket for something. Half dollars is getting scarce.

The only trouble with that was that Skeeter, good son that

he is, was then running down from where Lily and Minnie was to meet me. The sun caught the shine of that half dollar — and Skeeter saw it.

When he got to me, panting and smiling, he wanted one. Now I didn't happen to have another half dollar, but I didn't happen to want trouble either. I was already *in* trouble . What worried me the most was that the boys weren't too far from the van. How did I know whether big boobs wasn't still lolling in there with her crack wide open and drooling?

I'm not a crafty person, but I had to think of something. "Come on, boys," I said with a smile I didn't mean, trying to act like a scoutmaster, "We'll play a game for it — may the best man win."

So, even though my knees was barely up to it, I beckoned with a broad arm and got those boys jogging up the hill behind me as if it was army training.

The jog wore the boys out some, but not enough. It wore me out more. What was worse was that when we got to the top, I couldn't think of a game. "I gave the frying pan back," I told Lily, panting, playing for time. "I left it on the table."

"That's good." If Lily sensed anything about me funny, she didn't say it. Lily isn't a woman for conversation, except in emergencies. I knew it wouldn't do no good to ask her for a game.

Then I thought I had it. "Come on, guys," I said with a heartiness I didn't feel, "let's see who can jump the farthest. Armand, you give me that fifty cents, and we'll put it over there on that flat rock. You and Skeeter will do two jumps out of three, and whoever can do the best will get it."

Now Armand, he didn't like that. For so little, that kid was wily. "Let me keep it, George," he said, ramming his hands in his pockets, "until we see who wins it."

Well, I knew that wouldn't work, and I didn't like the little snipe calling me George neither. I guess Skeeter must have told him my name, but that didn't give him the right to call me by it, did it? Then there was the tinfoil too, and the mark on Skeeter's face.

"That won't do," I said. Then — sometimes I don't hold back when I should — I just came up behind that little kid and stuck my hands in both of his pockets and felt out that half dollar in his fist. It was in the left palm — warm and sweaty. He wriggled like an eel, but I got it.

Now maybe I was a bit rougher than was needed the way I am sometimes, because he cried, and just then — it was my luck, I guess — I caught sight of old Julien and his black-haired beauty Rose back at their table, where they were setting down the pink baby right next to the frying pan. Of course, they were looking my way.

Now as I said, I didn't want trouble. So I had to smile, and wave down at Julien as if it was all part of the game, and slip two sticks of gum I luckily had in my pocket, one to each. That's the way you get involved with things you don't mean to, things that aren't exactly truthful, but they seem like they're the only thing to do at the time.

Well then, I marked out a place where the kids would have to leap off the rock I'd peed behind for the fifty, knowing that Skeeter, who was more than a head bigger, would have to win. Armand wasn't crying by that time, and Julien wasn't peering up at us any more in that half-blind way he had. It looked as though I was going to get rid of the problem and be able to rest on the blanket and watch the last of the sunset, which was what I wanted.

It didn't work that way. I let Armand take the first try, so as to seem nice. Of course Skeeter beat him, maybe by not as much as I would have thought, but he did. On the second try, Armand did good for a kid his size, but I knew Skeeter would still beat him — no contest.

I had been marking the places the boys had jumped to with little stones, pebbles like the ones they'd been throwing before. Wouldn't you know that Skeeter, when it came to his second turn, would have to go and *land* on one of those little pebbles, poor boy, and slide off to the down side on his *face?*

Well, that ended it. I grabbed poor little Skeet up and headed towards where his mother was. And yes, I took that half dollar and gave it to Armand and headed him back to his folks and fireplace.

I guess Lily saw how I felt. As I said before, she's good. She and Minnie began to work on Skeet, who had scratched the same cheek where the stone had already hit him, and it was all right for me to go where I wanted to be. That was back on the blanket where I'd been before the other people came.

I got there. I stretched out. The sunset was done by then, but there was still the glow of red behind the dark pines. I should have just enjoyed it the way I usually did when we came to the Bull, but this time I couldn't. Mostly though, it was because of *where* I was in relation to the other people.

I'm a man that likes privacy. I keep shades down in the bedroom and the bath, would rather sit on the back porch out of sight than on the front in every fool's view. Where I was then, even though it was the spot I liked, was a spot where I was in full view of the out-of-staters. I could hear what they were saying, and if I decided to speak up, they could hear me.

Maybe it was because of what I'd done with the sister, but being up there in front of them like on a stage made me uncomfortable. Who wants to be the lion in the zoo? I didn't, so I got myself up and, taking the blanket, I went up behind where the boys had jumped — not where I'd peed nor where the sister'd stood, but further, almost where the drop off was.

It wasn't so comfortable there, because the moss ended, and

there was nothing but light green, mouldy-looking lichen and pale, stale tobacco-colored dust. I sat there anyway. In fact, I lay down almost, just propping myself on an elbow and opening the beer I'd thought to bring with me. The beer was a mistake, but I didn't know it at the time. I wasn't drunk after it, but I wasn't precisely sober neither. I guess you could have said I was mellow, and I would have stayed that way if the people down below hadn't gotten in an argument.

I couldn't see them from up there, and it shouldn't have been possible to hear them neither, but they were talking loud, in fact, shouting.

First Julien: "Don't tell me that, Rose!"

"It's true, I swear it to you!" she screeched.

"How could it be?"

"She said it."

"How *could* she?"

I began to get the uncomfortable feeling they were fighting about what I'd done with the dumb one, but I wasn't sure. I didn't feel right about what had happened, believe me, but after all, it was just one pop, and at the time it didn't seem likely the lady in question would be telling people stories.

Then, just as sudden as they'd begun, the voices stopped. Their baby was crying, but that was all. I peeked around my rock and saw that Lily had found marshmallows. I think we'd had them in the truck from another time. Skeeter, with his face patched up some more, was going with Minnie to get more wood for the fire, and Lily was sharpening some sticks with my jackknife I'd left on the table.

I got up for a minute and waved to them.

"Daddy's resting," Minnie said.

"Let him," Lily told her.

I did rest then, but not quite. There was something bothering me, but it wasn't voices from below. I lay there a while with my eyes shut before I figured it out. Then I knew. I'd been saving myself all day, not eating because of the picnic. We don't get steaks every Sunday. So after only eggs, I was still hungry. I'm a meat eater from way back. Bacon isn't enough.

When I knew that, I did drop off, but it wasn't a peaceful sleep. It was a dream the whole time — and not a good one. What I saw in my dream was a wolf, he was black. I had my shotgun, but he was running toward me, getting bigger as he came. I pumped him full of all the shot I had — in the chest, in the mouth, in the eyes — but he kept on coming.

The last thing in the dream was his mouth. It seemed to fill up the whole picture. His jaws were wide open, and I could smell the breath that came from them — not rank as you'd expect, but sweet, putridly sweet. It was like the perfume of the flowers at a funeral that are mixed — though you don't want to notice it — with something else. And from way back in his mouth, his pink tongue came lolling, moving slow as a pendulum from side to side.

I woke up then, but not because of the dream. I had the sense of things moving in the twilight, but I didn't know where. Something wasn't right. I was more hungry than before, but that wasn't what was the matter. It was something outside of me, something swirling around like the fire's smoke.

I stood up. The strange thing was that I couldn't see any-one — not the other people, not Lily and the kids. At first glance, it seemed the Bull had been picked clean.

Then I saw where everyone was. They were gathered around the other people's old blue van. Maybe it was because it was twilight, but I was still somewhat in the dream. Maybe too it was the beers and their snake poison on our eggs that were making me feel not right.

Anyway, I sort of stumped my way down the slope to where

they all seemed to be waiting for me as though I was someone special — Lily and my kids on the right and Julien and his woman and Armand on the left. His wife was holding the baby. The only one missing was the dumb sister.

They were all quiet. It was as if I, after sleeping up there, high on the horn, so to speak, was supposed to tell them something. Finally, it was Lily who stepped forward. "Julien's sister Ba is gone," she said. "She was resting in the back of the van — "

"Aunt Ba sleeps a lot," little Armand cut in, "she — "

The baby began to cry, but Rose shushed her.

"I told them you knew the Bull," Lily said, "that you could find where she's wandered to. It's getting dark, and Julien's got weak eyes. They never been up here before."

And they never should have come, was what I wanted to say, but naturally, I didn't.

"She isn't deaf and dumb only," Julien said in the queer way of talking he had, "in her mind, it is cloudy."

Yes, and it was getting dark. I knew what I was supposed to answer, but for a minute I must have stood there. Favors. God, how I hated favors. That was the way when you had to make space for people. People who didn't belong. People who got in the way. First *they* had to have the matches, then *we* had to have the pan.

Now they wanted their dumb sister, who had wandered off — maybe because of me, maybe not. Maybe too, they figured what she'd done with me was maybe why she'd gone. She had to have it: I was the chance one to give it. That meant I was obligated to find her now she'd lost herself, didn't it? Even though she might have wandered some place looking for more where there was no hope of finding, she was likely to be looking *anyway* — with her skirts high as a kite.

They were all looking at me. It was my turn for a favor,

wasn't it? Batter up. "I can get her," I said finally, "easier than a needle in a haystack." But when I did get her — that was what I didn't tell them — there wouldn't likely be a chance for me to needle her, now would there? So getting big Ba was going to be something I'd do out of the goodness of my heart. But the trouble was, I didn't *feel* good, I felt hungry.

Then Julien — he was standing downhill from me and that brought out the fact that he was little, truthfully, puny, besides being short-sighted — handed me the saddest little, the cheapest little flashlight you ever saw. It was all he had, I guess. Of course, I had to try it to be polite — as if it were worth trying. I knew from the way it looked it wasn't.

The flashlight didn't work. It was a throwaway, so I threw it — right down between us where a rock was so that the glass shattered and the plastic bounced. It just lay there, and he looked at it blank-eyed. He didn't try to pick it up.

"I have a lantern," I told him.

Why did I have to do him mean like that? I had to because I wanted to knock him down but didn't have proper reason, and couldn't anyway, because of the wives and kids. Of course, he was one of those fellows who isn't *worth* flattening, one of those little wormy ones who are always snaking their way into things, smiling and saying, "Thank you, *thank* you"; so that you have to do for them even though you'd surely love to grind 'em to juice and innards. Those types are so *pathetic* that you start to hate yourself for hating them, so you do and keep *on* doing. Then, when they've got all of it, and know you're tired and won't do more, they slither off. They know what they got from you — beside whatever it was they so dearly wanted — is *hate*.

The lantern I had in my pickup was the only light in the bunch — except that Minnie was carrying a little green lead pencil that lit up when you pushed the eraser. Naturally, those people hadn't planned for dark. So I told all of them to stay together by their fire while I went. Then, I didn't mean to let it, but it just burst out of me, I said: "Have you got anything else to eat?" Yes, if it was going to be favors again, I wanted something. Maybe it was the wolf dream — whatever the reason — I was ravenous.

Now it was rude to put it to them like that, wasn't it, with big boobs dancing around on the boulders somewhere? But then Lily, in that softening way women have, explained to Rose about how we'd left behind our steaks. Then Rose, who had a squeaky little voice when she opened up her beautiful red mouth, said there was something. So, giving Lily the pink baby to hold — I could see the women were getting friendly — Rose got a covered dish, a big one.

Right away, I wanted it. But then, when Rose took the top off, I saw it was nothing but a big fish lolling on its side with its head and tail and eyes and everything.

That was the kind of food people like that *would* have, I guess. My acquaintance with fish doesn't go much beyond tuna in a can, and I want to keep it that way. The ones with their bones and fins and teeth — you can keep all of them. I've always lived here by the mountains, but these people had to have come up from the shore.

I guess Rose would have been willing to give me that whole fish then and there, but my ribs weren't rattling *that* hard against my back bone, at least not yet. Polite as I could, I waved Rose off, but just to show she meant it, she passed Lily the fish when she took her baby back.

What I noticed then — it was something I shouldn't have noticed, but it was like the boobs, you couldn't but see it — was that the pinky porky baby looked a lot tenderer than the flat, skinny, silver fish did. It was just a thought, and I'd after all had my beers and eaten those eggs mixed with whatever it was from their snake meat. A few beers don't poison a man's mind, but who knows what was in that frying pan?

Lily, who is the same way I am about fish, gave the platter to Julien. Then Julien like a waiter — who knows, maybe that's what he was — came over to me with it and a long, crazy-shaped loaf of bread. "You take?" he said, blinking those blank eyes of his.

"No thanks." That's the kind of favor I hate most of all. They think they're doing you one, but you know you'd be doing them one to take it.

Julien gave me a funny look. Then he shrugged. "You would like to find my sister," he gave me an ugly little wink, "again."

He knew all right, and my smashing his flashlight hadn't helped. How'd he find out? I suppose it was sign language. Or was it something that had happened other times? Did he rent her out maybe with the van thrown in?

So the favor wasn't what it first looked: they'd give fish if I found Sister. The fish wasn't silver; it was tinfoil currency. The real deal was: if I found Ba, he wouldn't spill the beans to Lily.

So he had me, didn't he? And boy, I would have liked to have had him. I guess he saw that with those sea water eyes of his, 'cause I kind of bumped into the fish plate, and he kind of knocked it against me in a way that showed he would have liked to push it in my face. Then I got my hand on his wrist in a way you wouldn't call gentle, and then, maybe because Skeeter was right there and I didn't want nothing more with Armand, I didn't do more even though I could have just as well laid him out on the platter with the fish, pretty as a picture.

"Your boy threw a rock at my boy — hit his cheek," I said, mean as possible. "He bled. There could be a scar." I let go of him then, but I give his puny little arm a mean pinch before I did, to settle up. Then, the only one with the balls to set out in the dark, I went to determine where big tits had tiptoed.

The first place I went with my lantern, I guess because it would have been the easiest place to find her, was over at the east spot, opposite from ours. The picnic tables there had a broken plank, but that was all I saw. It hadn't been that way the year previous, from what I remembered.

From there — it was the only way — I toiled up to the north spot like a pilgrim, watching out for loose rocks and slippery little patches of lichen you could hardly see. By that time, hearing that giggly gurgle would have been a relief, but no Ba. Short for Barbara, I suppose. I said it out loud a few times, bleating it long and lonesome like as if she was the only thing in the world I wanted.

Truly though, what I wanted, maybe I shouldn't admit it, was the baby. Meat hunger, that's what it was. I've heard fellows talk about wanting pussy plenty, but I've never heard no one admit to hungering for just plain flesh. That one night though, I was a cannibal. Truth to tell, as I was stumbling around in the dark, bleating "Ba" now and then like a lost lamb, the mouth of my mind was on that infant.

That little pink-skinned thing had plump arms. I imagined the little legs would be plump too. If one was to stick a spike in between the legs and out the throat after striking off the head, roasting that little piglet would be easy. I imagined stoking the flames, I imagined setting the thing — which was just a comfortable size — to turn and sizzle. And thinking about that, I got to wondering — would the meat be white — or dark? Or mixed?

Then, in the midst of my cannibal ravening, I heard someone breathing, yes, panting, beyond one of the big north rocks. I thought of course it would be the dumb one, but it wasn't. When I shined the beam in that direction, I saw Rose.

"How'd you get here?" Hopefully it was too dark for her to see it, but I blushed because of it being *her* baby in my wolfish thoughts.

Rose held up Minnie's little green pencil flashlight.

"Oh. Why'd you come?" I asked, nervous, hoping she wasn't, beautiful as she was, wanting the same the other had. It isn't likely I'd have stopped for it, because what I was beginning to want more than anything was to go home to my steaks.

"I am here because she's here," Rose said.

"How'd you know?"

"I know things."

"Psychic?"

She nodded.

"My mother was like that." We stood there. "Show me then." I let Rose take the lantern from my hand. Without her saying nothing, I knew she knew about Ba and me, but even psychics don't know all of it. What they can see is like what you can see with a flashlight — just a portion of the dark, not broad daylight. I was willing to swear Rose didn't know I'd hungered for her baby in my mind.

When Rose shined my light at the biggest rock beyond the north fireplace, I groaned. That was where the sheer drop was. "Did she fall, Rose?" I even forgot about my stomach. I felt like crying. Poor dumb big boobs.

"Not yet," Rose said.

I didn't like that. I took a chill from her words. I grabbed my lantern back. It was as if the whole thing was planned to devil me — when all we'd wanted was a picnic — the place to ourselves.

Then, where Rose had had the beam pointing, there was Ba. She was facing us, and her long, messy, no-colored hair was winding around her in the evening breeze. Because I was below her, shining my light up, her boobs looked even bigger than before. Her dress — I was glad of it — was down to her ankles again.

"Ba," I called to her coaxingly, forgetting she couldn't hear me. But she could see me behind the flashlight couldn't she? In case she jumped, I raised my arms ready to catch her, while over my shoulder I told Rose: "Don't be here, you can't help."

I waited till I saw the little green pencil light going down the slope, too busy to wonder what was happening down there with Rose gone. The dumb one stayed still as a statue. I dropped my arms. The wind was raising her skirts up, but I didn't care, I had seen it all. All I wanted was for her to come down easy.

"Ba." I said it a couple times more.

Then, just once, I saw her work her mouth in the same way. It was as if she was saying it, but no sound came out. Actually, it was pathetic, because along with it she was crying. She cried big tears, she sobbed, but there wasn't hardly a gurgle. It was all silent.

Then I saw it was hard to be deaf and dumb with nothing nobody but a fool would want you for but your slit and your knockers. With the sadness of it, I almost cried with her, but then, I got hungry again. I was thirsty too. If I'd had the steaks that were sitting home in their shiny wrappers, I would have sucked them dry. Then, without barely chewing, I would have eaten what was left, raw. I wanted blood.

Wild as I was, it still seemed to me then that I was going to lead Ba back down the mountain and give her back to her brother — the last favor. I wanted that, to be rid of her, naturally, but another part of me felt sad and sorry. The sad side was: if she was nothing but cunt to me, I was the same — only a prick to her. It was pathetic when you looked at it. The sorry side was: my sin couldn't be hidden because Lily, if she didn't know already, was almost bound to find out.

I shouldn't have been thinking those thoughts then, I should have been paying Ba more mind. She wasn't that far above me, I could have gotten her. But then, darned if she didn't bolt in the other direction — heading for the drop off cliff.

I followed, but she'd taken dumb me unawares. She was quick, even in the dark. For sure, there was nothing wrong with *her* eyes.

She flew to that cliff like an eagle to her nest — and me hot behind her. There on the top by the big drop, I got her hand. I pulled her to me, we wrestled. Now I would have laid her again thankfully, just to quiet her, but she was too wild. She was a big woman. I had my head at her boobs, butting her, and then I got both of her hands in one of mine, but then she got me off balance and we both tumbled together to what I thought was kingdom come. We fell, but it wasn't where I'd expected or there'd be no story. Where we tipped over was only six or eight feet down instead of forty, but there were plenty of big rocks.

She was on the bottom, wedged between two rocks. I was on the top. She cushioned me except for my face. I took it on the chin. When I first knew I was alive after the shock of it, I was spitting teeth. I'd been hankering for blood, hadn't I? Well, I got a mouthful of it. It was my own.

Ba, poor dummy, might or might not have been breathing when I gathered her up limp and bloody. I felt for her heart, I think, but her boobs were so big, I couldn't find it. All I know was she was dead weight, and I got her out of there in the dark. Yes, I'd lost my lantern.

When I could see their fire, I called, but no one seemed to hear me. When I got near, I saw it was only Rose and the baby there — she was nursing it in the firelight. I could hear the kids playing a little ways off, and then Lily and Julien came from off to the side somewheres — maybe from the van, maybe not.

So I just plopped poor Ba on the picnic table among all the plates and cups, knocking over a big wine bottle somebody had been drinking. It spilled and bubbled red on the ground.

Then I dropped down on the bench because I was dizzy, and I started throwing up between my legs in the dirt. The spilled wine didn't smell good, and that made it worse. When Rose set the baby on the bench beside me to look at Ba, I just got sick all over again. That infant didn't look the slightest bit appetizing to me, and besides, she had a big one in her pants. I could smell it.

While I was spewing out the eggs, the bacon, the beer and everything else, with blood, till there was nothing left, they were trying to wake up Ba, feeling her head, rubbing her hands and feet. Lily, who I could tell had taken some of the wine they must have offered, started praying.

All the while they were trying to talk to Ba, and to feel her to see where she was broken, I knew there wasn't no point in it. She was dead, but I was too occupied getting up the last drop of bile to tell them. Finally, when there was nothing more to come from me but dry retching, I got up and tottered down to the stream. Washing myself wasn't easy, but there was an almost full moon rising, and that helped. When I rinsed out my mouth, I spit another tooth.

Then, like I had crossed death's river, I came back to them. By that time, Rose was standing aside in a way that said she thought Ba was gone — the dumb one's neck might have been broken judging from the way her head had dangled from my arms. Julien was beside Rose, holding the baby. Lily though, she was still rubbing Ba's feet, and the boys were holding Ba's hands — trying to help. Poor little Min was just standing by the fire, clutching her drab little doll in her arms.

Right off, I saw what was wrong with Lily and why she was doing so much rubbing. She was drunk, and it was worse with her than with me after the beers because she seldom took anything. She had been drinking Julien's poison-smelling wine.

So what did that mean? It meant that whatever Julien had or hadn't done to her — he wasn't worth killing. Instead, I was going to have to do him one last favor. An eye for an eye, a tooth for a tooth. I'd lost my teeth by his sister, but I wasn't going to ask him for his no-good eyes, now was I? Instead, I was going to have to help him — and that's exactly what I did.

It wasn't that I forgot my CB radio like the steaks, it was that I left the CB home on purpose because I wanted quiet. If I'd had it I could have called Mayday and had police and ambulance come, even at the Bull. But no CB, and it was a good twenty minutes winding down the dirt road to where the macadam began.

So what was the toothless wonder to do — send smoke signals? The answer was — the favor. So, taking Julien aside like he was a brother instead of a slimy sneak and a snake who'd given my wife drink and maybe even popped her, I outlined to him how we were going to get Ba in the van and cover her up with something — maybe the table cloth.

I told him that, and his wide blue eyes got wider. He was barely blinking, maybe he was in shock. What was in his mind didn't matter — as long as he did what I said. And that's just what he did do, with Rose getting together Lily and the children and leading them aside.

The doors of the van were still wide open, and I put Ba in there. Julien brought the table cloth — it was all there was. I kneeled in to lay it over the poor dumb thing, trying not to breathe much because the wine reek on the cloth could have easily made me sick all over again. As I did that, I have to admit it, my hand fiddled over her boobs once more. Maybe it wasn't right, but they were still warm. It was my way of saying good-bye, I guess. I knew I might never in my life get to feel another pair like hers.

Well, if you find a mess on a mountain top, you'll know it was from people like us. By the time I'd got back to their fire with Julien, Rose had gotten Lily and my kids into our pickup and was taking Armand and the baby to their van. They would sit in front.

Well, I kicked out what flames were left of the two fires, but apart from that, Julien and me, we didn't pick up anything. There were plates and cups, bread and wine — and we just left them there for the winds to blow, for the birds to pick.

When Julien was going — we were there by the coals of his fire — I was obliged, after all, to give him my address and name. For the police would be coming, wouldn't they? There would be an investigation. He took what I gave him and scrawled something for me on a napkin. What else was there to do?

Then, not far from the fireplace, I saw Minnie's doll. It wasn't worth taking, but something made me pick it up. Holding the half-unstuffed, ragged thing by its arms, I dropped it onto the coals. It caught. The fire flared up and burned like sunlight, but only for a little. After that, there was only the grey ash remembrance of the worn-out form.

Julien didn't say good-bye; I didn't either. We just went off to what we were driving and drove. He wound down the mountain first, and I came after, staying as far from what he was carrying as I could. When we finally got the Bull's bottom, he turned left and downhill, and I turned right and up.

Lily and the kids slept all the way home. I put all of them

to bed when we got there. The rest was easy, there was nothing in the pickup to unload. Yes, the steaks were there on the table, and I just shoved them in the refrigerator and slammed the door. I didn't eat a thing before I went to bed myself.

What was strange, afterwards, was that we never did hear from Julien. I expected police, questions, maybe even a deposition for a court. But nobody called, nobody came.

After a day or two, I thought to look for the paper napkin he'd put his name on. I found it — still in the pocket of my red plaid shirt. I unfolded it, and do you know, it didn't say nothing but three words: "Julien and Rose."

Now what could you make of that? Every night for a while after, I looked in the obituaries in the paper for a name that would be like Ba, but there wasn't one. Most of the women who died were old, and the ones who were young weren't called anything like Barbara. I asked Lily about it, and she said maybe they lived farther than we thought, way up north on the shore.

But how could they have buried her? I wondered. People would have asked questions.

Lily said maybe they went out fishing and floated her. True or not, the picture of her boobs above the billows flanked by silvery fishes stuck in my mind. We didn't say more about it. There are some things that keep a marriage happy, others that don't. I guess we both knew without saying so that it wouldn't be good to talk about that night, so that was it.

One thing. Minnie missed her doll and cried about it, so the next Friday I took her to the store and got her a pretty new baby in a pink frilly dress. I'd already heard what teeth would cost, but I felt obligated. Of course then Skeeter had to get something because she did. It was a game he wanted, the name of which I forget. That's all, hopefully. No more favors.

THE KILL

The Kill

It was time, time, time.

The last weekend in September was almost as warm as August, yet the white butterfly among the yellow chrysanthemums was fluttering feebly, unable to rise. A katydid drummed in the far corner of the garden, and, up the dark western hill where the sun was falling, a black flock of birds rose from the forest, circling south.

They were all standing on the back terrace of the plain white Connecticut former farmhouse — the family of the New York pediatrician and the girl. Of course, she was more than that. Both she and the doctor's son were well past thirty. For her, perhaps even for him, it was now or never.

The doctor, a stocky, broad-chested man, had changed into work clothes immediately after the Saturday afternoon drive from the city with his son and the fiancée. The doctor had been delayed all morning by a difficult case, but he was already holding a hoe.

51

"That animal," he announced, "he's been at the vegetable patch again."

"I knew it," said the mother, a thin, grey-faced woman who spent the summers in the country. "When I went to get peppers for the salad, I saw — " Her eyes, so dark it was impossible to distinguish the pupil from the iris, flicked like a whiplash in her son's direction.

The girl had been listening to the family all summer. She had been coming up for weekends ever since a friend had introduced her to the son in the late spring, yet she still found their conversations elliptical. Like a foreigner, she caught only partial meanings.

The son, who was restless, paced through the little circle and came to stand facing his mother, with the light at his back. In the beginning, there had been three brothers. The oldest had died at the age of eight in a school bus accident. The next, long divorced and childless, maintained a bachelor apartment in San Francisco. This son, the youngest, was well-spoken, polite, industrious, handsome.

He was ideal — everyone told her that. She was alone, without siblings, her parents gone. The advice of friends counted. Why then did she hesitate?

He had proposed almost immediately. She had accepted after a mid-summer's dance. In August, he suggested dates for the wedding — but she found fault with them. It was as though the decision in itself were unlucky; she could not bring herself to name the day.

"I want to make piccalilli before I close up the house and come back to the city," the mother was saying. "I'll need peppers — I wonder if . . . ."

The girl stopped listening. The mother had a way of going on for a long time about things that could have been said briefly. She had pricked her finger on a loose wire in the screen door as she came out. It smarted. Squeezing out a drop of blood, she sucked it.

"You'll have your peppers," the son said to his mother, almost rudely. He lit a cigarette, flicking the match precisely behind a red dahlia, where it would not show.

A spectator with the sun in her eyes, the girl saw how similar the two were. The mother's thin limbs, pale skin and dark glance were all repeated in him. His shadow stretched to mingle with his mother's at the door, by the steps.

With a wave of his broad, ruddy hand, the doctor turned away toward the vegetable patch at the far side of the house. Almost immediately, his wife went inside to cook dinner. The screen door slammed, and then, from the kitchen, came the clattering of pans.

There was one cloud at the horizon, and the sun slipped behind it. A cool breeze brought a few red maple leaves skittering across the terrace. The girl stood still and let the son approach her. The leaves whirled around their ankles, between their legs.

She hoped he would draw her away from the house, perhaps to the arbor where there was a wooden bench which had been part of a wagon long ago, when lands that were now lawns for weekend houses were still being farmed. The drive with his father had been tiring, the conversation formal. She wanted him to talk to her, to reassure her that —

"I have to go in for a minute," he announced, smiling down at her, telling her nothing. The screen door opened and shut. She heard his footsteps on the narrow, twisting stairs.

She was a special assistant in a private library which reopened in September after a summer hiatus. Exhaling, she sank down on the lounge where his mother usually sat. It was harder than she expected. Instead of springs, the lounge had a sheet of wood under its thin pad.

She twisted, then drew the pins so that her hair fell down long to pillow her head. Recently, since she was getting older, she had taken to binding the thick waves around her head.

The sun escaped the cloud. It grew warm again. The breeze died. A fly arrived, circled. She waved him away from the oozing crescent of blood under her nail . . . .

The son was before her, his shadow stretching the length of her body. Behind him hung the heavy boughs of the oak in the center of the lawn. The leaves were still green. She got up.

He had put on high boots, and the khaki shirt he always wore when they went to the woods — a hundred-acre tract which had escaped development because it was landlocked, a haven for deer, and perhaps, snakes. She would not be going with him this time, she saw. He was carrying a gun

"Do you like my hair down?" she tossed her head so red-brown curls undulated down her back.

"I like your hair." He set the rifle with barrel down against the white table at the corner of the terrace. He was careful about what he did — an engineer. Then he came over and kissed her. For a moment, she stared straight into his eyes — dark mirrors that did not reflect. Then her lids fell and she saw flashes inside them like heat lightning.

When she opened her eyes again, she saw above the dark straight strands of his hair a milkweed seed confusion of high, white clouds. The air was acrid, heavy with pollen. She coughed. When she began to bend at the knees and go limp, he released her.

Then, as in a film in which a series of frames was missing, she saw him striding up the hill towards the forest with the gun over his shoulder.

She was at loose ends. It was the mother's kitchen. It was the father's vegetable patch. Each would be friendly if she offered help, but it was not there she was needed.

She saw how the red sun inhabited the yellow field sloping up beyond the purple asters that edged the yard. She went beyond the flowers, between the forsythias, through the privet. She closed the gate behind her.

Beyond the fallen stones of an old wall rose the glistening, golden mound, a warm breast of the world. Above its shimmering grasses shone minute, hovering insects, humming, buzzing, breathing.

No longer farmed, the field, in the doctor's words, was merely mowed in the spring and left to itself. She ascended through ripe grasses, ochre stems crackling under her feet.

Grasshoppers rose from her path in winged, wide arcs. She smelled warm earth and, somehow imagining it would be soft as a loaf, threw herself down between milkweeds on the summit of the golden mound.

There was a rock under her stomach, a rough tuft of goldenrod at her feet, but she stayed, cushioning her head on her arms, tangling her hair with weeds. Her ear pressed to the drum of the ground, she heard the tapping of a woodpecker, the caressing cooing of a mourning dove. The high, even song of the insects was like anesthetic . . . humming . . . humming . . .

She opened her eyes after the thud of the first shot far in the forest. After the second shot, she sat up thinking of the uncoiling of a long, black snake. She did not want to be discovered, as it were, embracing the earth. People stretched out on the beach, but to lie flat alone in an empty field was —

Scrambling up, she hurried down towards the garden, catching her sleeve on a briar, wrenching her ankle on what seemed to be the long mound of a mole. Panting, she reached the terrace, pulling burrs from her hem, extricating a beetle from a curl.

Considering whether to arrange herself on the lounge as if she had been there all along, she heard her own heart — all the rest was white cotton silence. White curtains hung limply at the window of the quiet kitchen, and the doctor's hoe, neatly wiped of earth, was standing by the screen door. The mother and father often rested before dinner. She saw that the dark green shade of their bedroom window was drawn.

From somewhere down the road — sounds carried a long way in the country — she heard muffled laughter, and afterwards, a child crying. Then, footsteps returning from the forest through dry leaves.

She saw him coming down the path, a dark figure in the distance towering before the sanguine sun. No sound except his boots breaking brittle branches. The tomb white house was as silent as if they had already inherited the acreage.

Instead of waiting for him to come through his mother's

white chrysanthemums, she ran to meet him in the cornfield.
She saw he was carrying something.

It was limp. It was a claw-footed thing that dangled from
his left hand — long, furry, bloody, dark.

"It was in the trap," he told her as he came near preceded
by his slanting shadow, "but alive."

They approached the green, well-tended lawn together. She
stared at the ears, glazed eyes, sharp-toothed mouth — the
purple blood matted in the coarse, grey hairs. The red wound
in the midsection was edged with black.

He was holding the rifle with the barrel down. She could
smell the powder, the explosion. It was on his clothes, she
imagined, on his skin.

"The second shot — did a snake — ?"

"No. The mate was nearby. She got away."

"Oh." She watched the ticking dripping of the blood to the
earth. "What will you do with it?"

He shook his head, and then, silently, laid the body at her
feet.

Within herself, a dark place which had remained closed
opened. Like a stream finding its way, something was released.

He was looking at her, staring straight down into her face.
He reached for her hand. There was a bloody stickiness in his
palm — and perhaps her own finger was still bleeding. She did
not draw back.

The sun was going, leaving its rays above his hair. Behind
him, in the darkening woods, she imagined descendants amidst
yellow leaves. There was no counting them. They were shadows stretching all the way back along the trail of blood to the
heart of the forest.

"Shall it be October?" she asked, thinking it would be good
to have the day come before the cold.

He nodded, and, bending forward like a reaper, he picked
up the kill by the tail. With the gun set firmly under his
arm, barrel to the sky, he held her with one hand and the
animal with the other — and led her into the garden like
a conqueror.

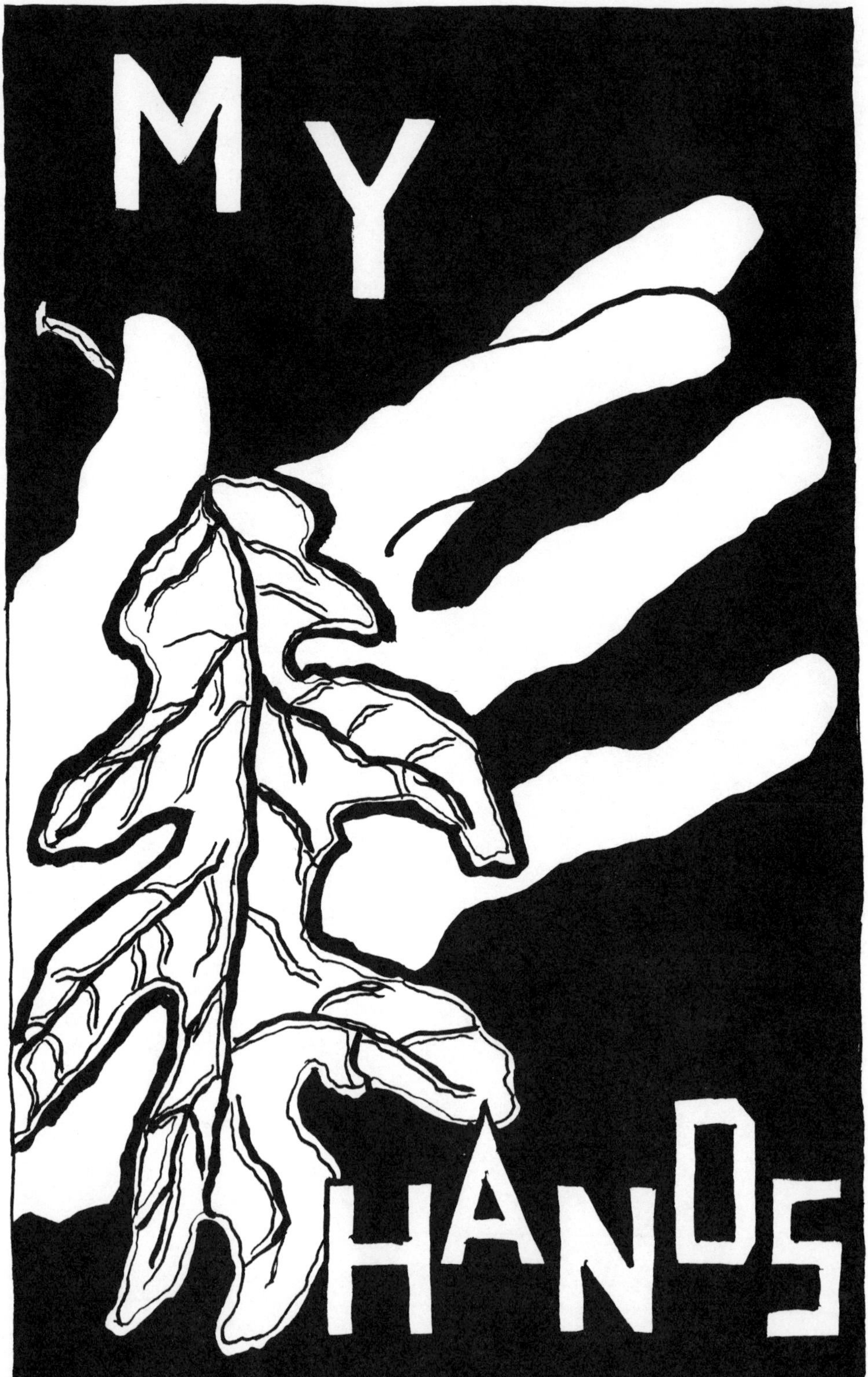
MY
HANDS

My
Hands

Sometimes, when I have nothing else to do, I look at my hands. There's nothing unusual about them. The fingers are long, a bit thin. The palm lines form an unexceptional pattern. On the backs, the blue veins are wavy, knotted. The nails are clean.

Keeping the nails clean is harder than you think. I'm a gardener — retired — but my fingers still crumble lumps of soil. They still pinch insects. They still graft and prune.

Gardens are the places my hands have been happiest. For a long time, I worked for the school on the hill. Then I got too old for their serpentine paths, their ceremonial beds, their ivy-encrusted bricks. I retired.

This is a small town. I've always lived here. I always will. When it's warm enough, when my fingers don't bend in ways

I don't want them to, I tend my own garden. My house is small and old, but my yard is deep and solitary. There are hedges all around, and the beds for flowers and the beds for vegetables stretch all the way back to the stand of hemlocks where the sun sets.

I live alone. My wife died ten years ago. No children. It's quiet in the evenings — sometimes too quiet. I get to thinking. I think about the things the fingers might do.

For instance, have you ever sat of an evening, after supper when time hangs heavy, and brought to mind the place where — in that one day — your hands have *been?* Even if *you* haven't gadded about — if you've stayed home, not even gone to the store — your hands have been, you might say, *everywhere.*

The hands have washed a body in the morning shower, made the coffee, pruned the roses, done a thousand other things the mind doesn't remember. What would you do without those long, faster-than-the-eye fingers?

Of course, hands can do other things. Once, on one of the summer Sundays my wife and I went out to the lake, I saw a young woman in a black bathing suit lying on her back. When she thought no one was looking (one hand was half-buried in the coarse brown sand, palm down) the other hand — it was the right one — slipped down the front of her bathing suit to smooth the skin of her breast, sliding back and forth over the nipple, then retreating.

When I saw that, my palms itched. My hands had to touch something. They were thirsty for it. Then the fingers did something that wasn't like them. They reached for a low branch of the maple sapling growing on the bank. In one stroke, they stripped the leaves, then wadded the moist fragments into a ball. The fingers clenched the green mass, and the nails made red half circles on the palm.

While the fingers were doing that I hummed. I always hum the same tune. It's a tune everybody knows, but I don't remember its name.

I don't punish my hands for things like that. Things like that don't happen often. This morning, though, there was an incident.

I was in the kitchen. From the kitchen window, you can see back to the hemlocks. I was looking out the way you do when spring hasn't come. You know it's too early for shoots to feel their way up through dead leaves, but you look for them.

For my age, my eyes are good. I can see things far off. It's the near things — like hands — that blurr. What I saw this morning from the window was a mound in the garden that wasn't there yesterday.

The mound was beyond the rhubarb bed back by the mulch pile in front the hemlocks, but it wasn't the mulch pile. The mound was new — it had risen out of the ground overnight like a toadstool. Toadstools are a law unto themselves. I've gone out of a spring morning and found topless, speckled toadstool towers high as your hand that weren't there the day before.

The mound, though, was more than toadstools. It was long as a barrow. It was light colored. I could see that much from the window, and when I got out there — I didn't stop to put my jacket on — I saw something else. Half hidden under brown leaves, something lumpy and tender was lying there. Strange indeed — but I didn't linger. There was a sharp wind blowing. While I shivered, the wind confirmed something.

The mound smelled mushroomy.

My palms itched.

It's been raining. I've been staying in. This morning though, I had to go out to the dentist. At the dentist's, my hands gripped the arms of the chair. When he was through, my hands were weak as babies.

When I got home — to be nice to the hands, to rest them — I strolled in the yard. It was nearly noon and sunny. It was getting warmer. There was no wind.

I saw that the mound was still there. I saw that the mound was rising. I saw that the mound was shrouded and blanketed with dark, wet leaves. What was underneath the leaves looked small and yeasty and soft.

With my hands in my pockets, I ruminated by the barrow. With my hands in my pockets, I stood still. Then — I didn't mean it to happen — one of my hands got out. It was the left one, and before I knew it, he had poked what was lying there. Just one finger, but it wasn't right. I made him stop.

Last night, it got warmer. When I went to bed, I opened the window. Just a crack. Then I got in bed and pulled the covers up. I tried to sleep.

There's a certain smell mushrooms have. Toadstools the same. Maybe the smell is like fallen trees in the woods, turning to splinters and sawdust. Maybe the smell is like something else — something female. Anyway, it's a smell that stays in the back of your nose. You can blow your nose, you can wipe your nose — but the smell is still there.

As I was lying in my bed, trying to sleep, that smell came right into the room. I knew where it was coming from. I knew what was lying out there — growing.

This morning, I stood at the kitchen window. I had eaten, but my hands were hungry. My hands were rubbing themselves. The left was rubbing the right, the right was rubbing the left. My hands wanted to go out.

It was raining. I put on my jacket. I put on my thick-soled boots. The ground was soft. My thick-soled boots made kissing sounds — sinking down, rising up. A garden isn't just what you can see. A garden is just as much what you can't see — lying underneath, stirring.

That's the way the mound was. Rising from underneath, the mound was ripening. She was lying face down. She was lying with her arms over her head. What was beginning to be her hair — broken twigs, bits of old leaves turning soft and black, bodies of summer bugs frozen hard with their little legs curled tight — was garlanding over her shoulders, wreathing down her back.

I squatted beside her. My hands were quiet. I was quiet. We didn't touch. Then we went inside.

It wasn't until I was washing my hands for lunch that I saw the spots. There were two on the left hand. There was one on the right hand. The spots were pale — the color of a fungus. That's what comes of poking.

Maybe what I have on my hands *is* a fungus. Today, there are more spots. The spots don't itch, the spots aren't sore. The spots are nothing but toadstool speckles — but they don't wash off.

It rained for two days, it rained for two more. It was a slow rain, a rain that showed things were growing. It isn't time for tulips or even crocuses, but things are happening. My hands are covered with spots.

It's almost noon. I can see the sun today. The sun is sliding between watery clouds. I haven't been out, except to the store. I haven't been out in back. But now I am putting on my jacket and my thick-soled boots. I am opening the door.

Out. Out to the barrow. I can smell the mushroom smell. I can see her. She is lying on her back.

I can't stay out. I have to take my hands inside.

Inside is no better. My hands are getting out of hand. My hands are buttoning and unbuttoning the buttons of my shirt. My hands are playing with what hair I have left. My hands are doing other things I won't mention.

What can I do about it? My hands are taking the cups down from the shelf. My hands are running their speckled fingers around the edges of the cups. I don't like that. I have to drink from those cups.

We are at the point where my hands are telling me what to do. We are at the point where I am doing it. Because the knuckles are knocking at the window panes, I get my jacket. Because the nails are scratching at the screeching glass, I get my thick-soled boots. Because the spotted fingers are so tight on the knob, I let them open the door.

Snap your fingers. That's the time it takes to get to the mushroom mound. The mound smells mushroomy. The smell gets into my nose and stays there.

We are bending over the mound. In the shadow of the hemlocks, she is toadstool color. She is smiling. We are dig-

ging. She is smiling. We are delving. My spotted old hands are
reaching, grasping —

I WON'T LET THEM!

My boots take over. You remember my boots. My boots
have thick soles.

KICK.

KICK.

KICK.

You might call it dancing.

KICK. STOMP. KICK.

I hum as an accompaniment. I hum my little song. I even
sing it.

"Tra-la. Tra-laaa."

There is nothing left but dark leaves, spotty toadstool
crumbles and hemlock shadows. I can see that from the
kitchen window. As I said, I can see things better at a distance.

I have taken my limp little hands inside. I am washing
them carefully in warm soapy water.

I am a nice man. Nice.

The spots on my hands are gone. It has stopped raining.
Today, I looked out the window and saw the first crocus.

My hands are fine. They do what I want. My hands don't
make a move without me. To prove it, I take them out to the
barrow. The barrow isn't there. What was a mound is now as
flat as the other beds.

Wait.

There *is* something there, something I can't see very well.
I can see well enough though to see it's something growing.

What is growing is small — no bigger than nipples or finger tips. There are a lot of little ones, poking straight up. I'm not sure, but I think they are speckled.

I hear the telephone ringing. We get inside in time to answer it.

It is the dentist. He is calling to confirm the next appointment. I haven't forgotten the next appointment. I am old, but I don't forget. I haven't forgotten to keep my hands clean. I haven't forgotten that toadstools are a law unto themselves.

To show I haven't forgotten, I hum my little song.

Horse and Cart

It was the kind of quiet country place where people put cart wheels on their front lawns and grew petunias between the spokes. The old streets were laid out around the square in a grid that had fewer crossings than a checkerboard. Winnona's house was on Elm just around the block from the convenience store and Fran's Beauty Parlor.

On an October Monday, the first since the annual change from summer daylight to winter time, Winnona was finishing the breakfast dishes. Then, as she was cleaning the crackled blue and white egg cup that her husband Sam used every morning of his life, she sensed the sun's unfamiliar lateness and parted the green checked curtains over the sink to let in more light. Outside, along the block lined with ancient maples turned orange and red, there was something awful funny moving through the long morning shadows, the spinning-down leaves.

It was, of all things, a horse and cart. Pert as you please, the dark contraption was rumbling along where such a thing hadn't been, most likely, since the Sweet Hill Dairy went over from milk wagons to trucks toward the end of the Second War. When Sam came home with his leg shot up and they got married, she remembered, you could still smell that old white milk mare sometimes on summer mornings.

This horse was piebald grey and white, and the high wheeled wagon he drew was long and narrow like a Conestoga. Open and uncovered, the rattling wreck was piled to the sky with dirty-looking bundles bulging with what could have been anything from coal to spuds to the castoffs of a whole churchyard full of folks who wouldn't be needing them now, thank you. Above the rags, rubble or whatever you pleased to call it, was a man raised on the buckboard wearing a battered top hat. The raggedy creature — old as the hills and stiff as straw-stuffed figures set out on porches for Halloween — sat with his knees spread and his hands held wide and high, clutching the reins as if life depended on it.

Winnona had been intending to sweep the porch anyway. Drying her hands on her apron and leaving the cups and saucers in the sink, she grabbed the broom from the closet and let the screen door slam behind her. A large, slow fly rose from the papery tan hydrangeas beside the railing, circled her head, floated west. The horse and wagon came even with the privet hedge that hid Sam's vegetable patch. The unexpected coot of a coachman took no notice of her standing pretending to sweep the top step gaping, but then, after she'd seen the rusty sheen of age across the shoulders of his long black coat, he looked back. His hair was yellowish white, streaming to his shoulders like chaff in the wind. His eyes seemed empty as glass.

Rag picker, scissor sharpener, deranged old dirt farmer —
he had to be somebody like that. No, she wasn't anything for
him to rein for — a dumpy, brown-haired woman in a damp
apron. He measured her like a sack of nothing at all.

The wagon rolled on past the rotted elm stump at the far
side of the driveway. Winnona saw dented shovels and a rusty
scythe sticking out crazily behind where they could catch in
an iron clad wheel. And where, when the dump was at the far
end of town in the opposite direction, was he going anyway —
to kingdom come?

Winnona reversed the broom and began to sweep leaves in
earnest, following the wind-swirled eddies across the porch and
forcing them down the steps.

A pickup passed, braked behind the wagon, went on its
way toward the overpass that bridged the old tracks. There was
still one freight a day.

The wagon was out of sight, but someone had lost a pumpkin in the middle of the pavement — smashed to smithereens.
The phone was ringing. Winnona went in.

She expected it might be the hospital where she was a volunteer visitor, but instead it was Bobo Tompkins across the
street.

"Did you see him?" Bobo demanded breathlessly. A part-
time reporter for The Blytheville Blade, she had a way of making everything sound like a headline.

"Ay-eh," Winnona told her evenly.

"He's one of 'em."

"One of which?"

"You haven't heard? It's been coming in over the wires at
work. There's a bunch of them — farmers failed on their farms
and foreclosed, homeless people from down the river, maybe
even crazy people coming on one-way bus tickets from cities
that don't want to take care of them. They're having a gath-

ering out at the flats."

"The flats — ?" That was where Sam and his partner Phil
were building six speculation houses in cornfields from family
farms they'd inherited way back from his side or hers, she
wasn't sure which.

"Well no, not *at* the flats. It's not beyond the flats at the
river — the old Mullaney land by Mile High Hill. Call me
tonight. Maybe I'll have more on the story. I've got to take the
kids now." Bobo, who was always in a hurry, hung up without
saying good-bye.

Bobo had two little boys, both too young for school. She
took them to the day care place in what once had been the
First Methodist but was now painted pink and blue with
swings and slides set out beside the old burying place.
Winnona wondered whether Mary Lou, her daughter who had
been married ten years and was now expecting for the first
time, would do the same. Nobody stayed home any more. She
herself had "graduated" from ladies' circles a few years back
and started in at the hospital.

The phone rang again. "Are you going today?" There was
no need for the caller to identify herself. Peaches Rosewell
wasn't Winnona's oldest friend, that was Celladina Thorpe
that she'd known since third grade, but she and Peaches, who
was her same age, talked on the phone every day.

"Nobody called to make sure, but I'm going over as soon as
I finish the dishes. I don't want to miss Mr. Barker. Do you
want a ride?" Peaches volunteered at the hospital too, but she
wasn't a visitor. Peaches did beautification — hanging pictures
in the halls and arranging flowers in the waiting rooms.

"No, I'll take my own car. I have to leave early. There's a
meeting at church about what's going on out at the river.
Celladina and some ladies are getting together clothes and
things to eat. One poor fellow just dragged through town in a

dray. Did you see him? He was driving a rattleboned paint and pale as death."

Winnona allowed she had. "A bleached out scarecrow and good riddance — " she burst out. Then, ashamed of her own meanness, she added: "But the horse was another story — I grew up on a farm, you know. Given the chance, I believe he'd go with the wind."

After she hung up, Winnona finished the dishes. Then she didn't even think of anything like the horse and cart again until she was on the third floor of the hospital on her way to Mr. Claude Barker's room at the end of the hall.

Stopping at the water fountain, she couldn't help noticing one of Peaches' framed pictures above her head. "The Angelus." It was an old fashioned thing you were supposed to like because there was a farm couple in the center, praying. Winnona had a contrary streak. What she liked was the field where they were standing with their little barrow, in particular, the way the light rolled along the furrows — and maybe cart ruts — behind them.

The door to Mr. Barker's room, she saw when she got there, was almost shut. That wasn't a good sign. In the time she'd been a volunteer visitor (two or three mornings a week for terminal people who didn't have anyone but the nurses to look in on them) Winnona had got to notice little things. It wasn't good either that Mr. Barker, an old widower farmer who didn't have anyone to come to him but a daughter with young kids who lived two hundred miles up river, was lying down flat as a pancake at ten o'clock in the morning. Usually, even the worst-off ones had their beds rolled halfway up after breakfast.

Weakly, Mr. Barker opened his eyes and raised the fingers of one hand in what was meant to be a wave. He was dying of cancer of the esophagus. His nourishment came from a plastic bag on a steel pole standing at the side of his bed. A pale, bubbling fluid descended through an "S"-shaped tube into his arm. Sometimes he still attempted to take water from a paper cup, but it was like swallowing a stone.

Winnona had been his visitor since August when he came in from his furnished room over the hardware store. First a farmer and then a dairy farmer, Mr. Barker's last hundred acres and his two hundred milking shorthorns had had to be sold off after feed went sky-high. He and his wife moved into town, but then, she upped and died.

Winnona went to the corner by the window to get one of the pine folding chairs kept for visitors. The other chair was hardly used. Mr. Barker's two sons had been killed in Vietnam, and his daughter had only come down once with all her kids, on a Sunday afternoon the first month he was in the hospital. It was Winnona who had brought and watered the pot of yellow chrysanthemums on his window sill. She had also put the sepia studio portrait of his wife, and the blurry snapshot of the grandchildren that the daughter had left, on his bulletin board with thumbtacks. Winnona brought him shaving lotion that Sam had been sent by cousin at Christmas and didn't like the smell of — and tissues that were better than the skimpy little squares in small boxes that the hospital gave out.

The room looked fine, Winnona reflected with a certain satisfaction, but Mr. Barker didn't. Unfolding the chair on his good side — one ear was better than the other — Winnona smoothed the sheet.

"Kin ya talk?"

"Yep." The machine made a sucking sound. He didn't say anything more. It was a good while since Farmer Barker had trod his fields, but his face still bore the marks of the sun. There were deep furrows down along the sides of his mouth.

Sometimes, Mr. Barker's mind wandered. On good days he knew he was old and in the hospital, on other days, he didn't.

Whichever it was, he talked about his old acres. His wrinkled old brown-spotted body was in a white hospital bed, but his mind was on his farm.

"I was jest standing there," Mr. Barker began without introduction , "looking down towards the stream, and I got to thinking — "

Settling back with a dead leaf she had plucked from the chrysanthemum still in her palm. Winnona let him go on with the story that she could have told herself because she had heard it so many times. It was about how — fifty or sixty years ago when he was young — he had decided to buy the fields adjoining, almost doubling the size of his farm.

" — and I thought to myself," he went on in a whispery voice, "that I could have land as far as the eye could see, all the way down to the river and up to the pines."

Suspecting that the doubling of the property might have been what caused him to go under in the end, Winnona also knew he didn't see it that way. Dying people, Winnona had discovered, could set their minds on a thing. Merrill, the seven-year-old foster-home girl who had died the previous spring of leukemia, had talked again and again of a doll in a purple dress her mother gave her just before she and her father got killed in a car wreck.

Another one, Natasha, the beautiful Russian ballet dancer all broken up in a bus accident on her way to Chicago, remembered her debut in Leningrad — the applause, the warmth, the colored lights. Of course, her folks couldn't get through from Tbilisi, so Winnona was with her most of that last week. It was first time she had been with a person when death came.

Later, Winnona saw the worst part was the loneliness. Nurses and other people would say you looked well when you didn't. No one would *admit* anything. But there was no fooling the dying — they *knew*.

Farmer Barker fought to swallow — and won. "By supper-time, my mind was set on it. Those acres was meant to be mine — make no mistake. When I come back to the house, Mary told me she was expecting again. It seemed like a sign — "

His voice trailed off. Winnona felt his weakness as if it had been her own. It had been the same with the others. You had times you'd be willing to drain your own blood into them even though you knew from the beginning it wouldn't help. Whether Farmer Barker could go on talking or couldn't didn't matter. She knew it all by heart — and more.

As it turned out, he didn't get a chance to go on. A nurse came in to give him a shot, and right after that, he drifted off. After watching by him a while, Winnona went home.

On the way home, she took the windy way through the truck farms instead of the main road everybody used. When you got tired of things, open land calmed you. Woods were good too, but tilled fields were best. The even rows — whether it was time for sowing or reaping — seemed certain and satisfying, like the refrain of an old song everybody knew or a hymn in church.

One of the summer farm stands was still open, so she stopped and got some real apples — dull and normal looking instead of all waxed up and tasteless — and a good-sized pumpkin. It had been a long time since she'd made pumpkin pie. Just standing there, getting the smell of the soil, made her feel good. But then, after she'd come back and around the square and turned into Elm, she saw something bothersome.

Maybe it was because of the way the sun was — slanting in her eyes in a wintry way — but it seemed in the rear view mirror that there were marks on the pavement. Thin, silvery trails that could have been left by a wagon gleamed — and then disappeared as she turned into the driveway.

Whatever it was, Winnona wasn't set to dwell on it. She needed to start her New England boiled dinner, something she hadn't fixed in a long while but ought to have because it was Sam's favorite. Hospital visiting put you in mind of things like that. She and Sam were both healthy as horses, but still, it was good to do such things when you could — in case later was too late.

It was a good dinner. Afterwards, Winnona and Sam put on sweaters and sat on the front porch to watch the harvest moon come up — something they hadn't gotten around to all fall. Sam, who would have been to college and maybe even to engineering school if it hadn't seemed too late when he came home from the war with a leg that would never be quite right, knew about constellations — easy-to-see ones like Orion and ones that were hard to find like Pegasus — and vegetable gardens and a lot of other things besides contracting and building. A few nights off, he told her, it was going to be a blue moon.

"Don't look blue to me tonight," she told him. "It's corn-kernel yellow and getting fuller."

"That's not what a blue moon means," Sam said, "but nobody knows it. It isn't the color. A blue moon is when you have two full moons in the same month. It only happens every two or three years."

"Oh — " Winnona never got tired of hearing Sam talk about things like that he'd read in the papers or someplace else. He was a big man, but he had a quiet voice that was good to listen to. She reached for his hand.

"The moon was full at the beginning of this month, and she'll be full again come Halloween," he explained.

Winnona began to wonder whether particular things were supposed to happen when a blue moon was on its way — like

times when there was an eclipse or a comet nobody'd seen for
years. She was getting ready to ask, then the phone rang. Sam
went in. Evenings, unless it was Mary Lou long distance from
Cincinnati, calls were almost always business.

Winnona stayed alone on the porch, listening to the crickets sing in the willows. It was Indian summer. The air was so
bland and soft she began to feel warm. Slipping her sweater off
and wadding it in the small of her back, she made the old
porch glider swing slowly, back and forth. After a while, she
got up and stood at the top of the steps, looking down the
silent street.

There was nothing in the road at all except darkness. The
big, blotted night shadows below the branches of the trees
extended all the way down to the street lamp beyond the fire
hydrant.

She could hear Sam, still on the phone. A woman on the
other side of town wanted a new roof. Winnona decided to go
up to bed.

Later, after she had gotten under the covers and turned out
the light, she had to crawl out again over Sam's side to open
the window wide. It was so close, the glass curtains were barely
moving. Then, when she was lying down again with all the
blankets thrown back, she heard something.

It could have been Sam putting down the windows on the
other side of the house, but it sounded more like a cart going
in the same direction the other had taken. Rattley bump.
Winnona did not open her eyes, but she was almost sure she
heard slow measured hoofbeats. They were faint as the tapping
of a fly against a window pane, yet close as fingertips drum-
ming on her pillow.

Later, when she was almost asleep, Sam came into the
room and got undressed without turning on the lights. He
didn't say anything. Instead, as he had done so many times

before, he kissed her, took her by the thighs and pressed himself on top of her. Afterwards, he rolled a little to the side, but they did not disentangle. They slept contentedly in each other's arms.

The next day after breakfast when Sam had left for the flats, there was a call from the hospital. Mr. Barker had had a bad night. Tuesday wasn't one of her days, she came Mondays, Wednesdays and sometimes Fridays. They knew that, but they had been calling his daughter's house and couldn't get an answer.

"I'll be over," Winnona told the floor nurse. She had a standing ten o'clock appointment Tuesdays at the beauty parlor, but Fran would understand. She had also promised Sam she'd drive to the flats to see where he'd started the first house, but she could go afterwards.

On television, as she cleared the breakfast leftovers and stacked the dishes in the sink, there was news about an Iowa farmer — a nice looking man from his picture — who had shot the bank man and then himself when his mortgage was foreclosed. It was a blonde girl with hairspray telling about it, and Winnona doubted she'd ever been on a farm.

To fortify herself — there was something in her holding back from going — Winnona poured a glass of milk. It was the last of the carton — she'd have to remember to stop at the convenience store. Because most everything was dirty or in the dishwasher, she took an old cottage cheese glass from the back of the shelf. Glasses like it — or maybe even this very one — used to come on the milk wagon with the bottles of milk and cream. The milk wagon had rubber tires, but you would hear the heavy hooves in the dark — and then the raised-letter bottles and the cheese glasses with Disney animals on them being lifted from the metal basket. If you'd forgotten to leave a note in the neck of an empty bottle for something extra you needed, you might tiptoe downstairs in your bathrobe and see the inside of the backed up cart.

There was always spilled milk in there, Winnona recollected, trying to galvanize herself to get her coat, and in the winter the milk froze to a thin film. The sour smell mingled with the sweet smell of the horse's hay and the wet wool smell of the horse's thick grey blanket. The milkman had a jacket made of the same wool. Both had round green emblems that said, "Sweet Hill."

The milk now was too cold. As she drove to the hospital, it was like a clenched fist in her stomach. The milkman's milk was warmer when you took it in, more digestible. It was silly to wish things had stayed the same, but today's milk without cream at the top and even cream itself, white and thin and filled with something like formaldehyde to make it last a month instead of whip, was, as Sam might have said, a horse of a different color.

As soon as she stepped through the door of Farmer Barker's room, Winnona sensed it. Everything was the same — he was still lying there with the tube feeding him, the chrysanthemum was still on the window sill, the photographs were still on the bulletin board — but there was something in the room that hadn't been there the day before.

Deliberately, Winnona marched to the corner, got the folding chair, set it in the usual place beside him. Without asking, she knew he couldn't talk. His breathing was slower, his IV seemed to be running faster. His eyes were shut. There was a new machine on the other side of his bed, one of those things that turned your heartbeats into jagged hills and valleys. While Winnona was settling herself, a nurse came in and checked the heartbeat machine.

After the nurse was gone, Winnona took hold of Mr. Barker's hand. It surprised her when it gripped back pretty hard. Then, one of his eyes opened up. Even though the other eye wasn't working, Winnona could see he was looking at her. Then his mouth gaped. He was trying to say something, but he couldn't.

Winnona wasn't one to let such things bother her. She held on. She knew she could say what his mouth couldn't. "You were standing up on the hill," she began conversationally, going back to where he had been the day before. "You had set your mind to get all the acres — "

Something happened in the hand that Winnona was holding. It moved in a way that told her this was what Mr. Barker wanted. He wanted her to talk for him. He wanted her to say the things he couldn't.

And so she went on, taking it easy, going through the part about his wife and the daughter she was carrying for him. "There was a breeze blowing as you came down the field to your house," Winnona told him. "It was spring and you could smell the wet soil — the furrows where the seeds had been put in. Your wife had dinner waiting, and the land was going to be yours as far as a body could see — and beyond." Winnona paused.

If a hand could sigh, Mr. Barker's did so. After pressing her fingers, it opened.

Right away, Winnona knew. The machines were going on, but Mr. Barker wasn't. That was all right. She just sat there. The room began to empty out. Things got quiet. The heart machine wasn't working any more. As if to free what had to go, Winnona got up and opened the window. The sun was very, very bright, and in the yellow-leafed oak under the window, she saw a bird with red on its wings.

Behind her, the door of the room opened. It was the nurse,

and behind her, the doctor resident. Behind them came a plump stranger that had to be Mr. Barker's daughter from the photograph.

Winnona didn't say anything. She was hoping that they weren't going to do the pumping and pounding and bell ringing they sometimes did.

Perhaps they might have — Winnona wasn't sure afterwards — but just then Mr. Barker's daughter dropped right down on the floor like a lump of dough. So, by the time they had got the fainted woman up again, there wasn't much choice but to cover the old man with a clean sheet.

Half facing the bed and half facing away, the woman sat in the folding chair, sipping the glass of water they had given her. There were tears oozing out of the corners of her eyes into little wrinkles at the tops of her cheeks.

"I wanted to get here sooner," said the daughter, whose name was Marjorie. "I had my littlest boy at the doctor's this morning. He's been coughing — " she broke off.

After a while, Winnona and the nurse got Marjorie out of the room and down the hall to the place where there was a couch for visitors. Marjorie was crying hard, but after a while, she wasn't so bad.

After the nurse went, Winnona told her: "He died peaceful."

"I should have come sooner," Marjorie said. "I wanted to, but with four kids — it's always something." She began to cry again.

Winnona nodded. "You did what you could. There was no saving him, you know."

"I know." Marjorie wiped her face and blew her nose. "I'm expecting again," she confided after a pause. "I guess that's why I passed out so sudden. It's my last one. I'm forty."

"Your father would have been pleased, I'm sure. I know it

made him happy — your mother having you — "

"You know, if it's another boy, I'm going to name him for my dad."

"Good. He'd have liked that."

Winnona looked at her watch. It was already after two. She was beginning to feel tired. "I'm afraid I'll have to be going," she told Mr. Barker's daughter. "I promised my husband I'd meet him out at the farm." She stood up. She meant to say the flats, but it came out like that and she didn't bother to correct herself. After all, it had been a farm once.

"I want to thank you," the daughter said, standing up too and taking Winnona's hands. "A nurse wrote a couple of letters for him. He mentioned you."

The need to leave the hospital grew in Winnona. There was no window open in the sitting room, the air was dry. She ached to be outside. Also, she was afraid the daughter would want to talk to her about what people always called "the arrangements." Winnona didn't favor visitors getting involved in such matters. All she could help with, she'd decided, was what came before. What came after was other people's business. Visitors, she'd concluded, shouldn't go to funerals either. It was the job of a visitor to go as far as you could with somebody, and that was far enough.

In the hospital parking lot, Winnona felt a difference in the air. It was colder, winter was on its way. Some years, the first snow came in October. After starting the car, she moved the lever from "COOL" to "WARM" and turned on the heat for the first time since spring.

If she hadn't promised Sam, she would have stopped for a hot cup of coffee with somebody or gone straight home. Lights were on at Peaches' Dutch colonial, and the car was in the drive at Bobo's split level. Instead, Winnona went on — straight out Elm, the route the cart had taken. There were no wagon tracks on the road.

After crossing the hump of the old railroad bridge, she sped by what was left of Landfill Apple Orchards, and then, past the old Murchison place where the road narrowed. The Murchisons were all died out, but there was still somebody living there, she saw, even though the windward side of the barn was caving in and the top of the silo had blown off into the corn field. Whoever the poor souls were in the unpainted house with its porch propped up, they had kids. There was a pumpkin in the front window, and someone had tied plastic bags to look like ghosts in the scrubby little tree by the mailbox.

Sam had a sign that said "Winfield Gardens: Luxury Homes," but Winnona went a little beyond by mistake. She turned around where there wasn't much shoulder because of the culvert that followed the road to the river. If one of the carts coming this way caught a wheel in a place like that, she reflected, it would take the very devil to right it.

The dirt road that Sam and Phil had cut across the furrows led to what was going to be a nice dead end street with a circle of custom built houses and a landscaped turn-around. Right now though, there was nothing to see but construction machinery, trucks and big piles of dirt.

Pulling in behind Sam's jeep in case the ground was soft in other places, Winnona saw how grey the sky was getting. There was rain on the windshield, and beyond the drops of water — not a living soul. Where was everyone?

"Hallo — " Sam was somewhere, calling to her.

Then, in a hillocky place beyond a pile of stones, she saw his head and shoulders. A smiling sexton, he rose, as if from Golgotha, shouldering a spade. "Come and see it — " He limped toward her, beckoning, a jolly brown-jacketed figure against the pale sky.

Sam helped her over the rough ground, and when they got there Winnona saw that everyone was down in the bottom — Phil and the two men who were regular helpers. Walled with cinderblocks, it was the long, rectangular cellar of the first house. To get into it, you had to go down a rickety-looking ladder.

"Tomorrow," Sam told her, "if it doesn't frost up on us, we'll pour the concrete floor."

What was down there now, Winnona saw, acknowledging the waves of Phil and the others, was plain old dirt pressed flat as the palm of your hand. The cellar wasn't unusual except that it was very long. The house, she could see, was going to be grander than others Sam had built.

He was ready to hand her down the ladder, but Winnona resisted, shaking her head. "It's dark in there — " she told him, and truthfully, the corners were crowded with dank shadows. The sun was dropping. She didn't fancy the idea of going down the ladder and having to climb out.

"You came so late — " he questioned. "I thought you'd be here before noon."

"They called me from the hospital," she explained. "It was Farmer Barker."

"Gone?"

She nodded.

"Well, it had to be, didn't it?"

"It did." Their eyes met. "I guess I could make it down after all," she said.

The ladder was shorter than it looked. Once down, the only thing was to admire the neatly stacked courses of cinder blocks rising twelve high and to smell the mortar. Still, the way the cellar was struck her, she couldn't think why. A long, rectangular place open to the sky. . . . Then she knew.

A time back, in the Sunday supplement, there had been

pictures of an old place they were digging up in China. Big as life pottery soldiers had been taken out of the earth, and horses too. They had even, yes, that was the picture she remembered, found a whole horse and cart and maybe a driver too in a place the size of this.

It was raining. Winnona told the men how fine the cellar was and said good-bye.

"You look tired out," Sam said when he had helped her up the ladder and was walking her back to the car. "Were you there when he passed?"

She nodded. "He went easy."

"That's good." He thought for a minute. "Since it's too late to pour the floor now, we're letting the men go early. How'd you like to have dinner at the Chinese place on the square? It's a while since we've been out."

"I'd like it fine." She coughed. The rain was coming down inside her collar in back. The thought of not having to cook dinner was more of a relief than she expected — her throat was scratchy.

"You go on home and freshen up," Sam told her. "I'll be along." He took her hand, squeezed it, then let it go.

Driving home with the heat turned to "HIGH," Winnona knew Sam thought she felt down about Farmer Barker. That wasn't so. In point of fact, she was glad for the old man. What did trouble her mind, maybe for no good reason or maybe because the two days at the hospital had worn her just as Sam said, was the horse and cart — not the one they'd found in China in a cellar or somewhere — the one, and maybe others, that had come by the house.

It was the out-of-placeness that bothered her. For better or no, things were meant to go forward — not back. That old spectre and his rig, carting bags of wind or whatever, were as out of place as if the milkman had started bringing his wagon round again.

It rained all night, but in the morning there was sun. One more day, at least, of Indian summer. Winnona usually took time off after somebody passed. It took some while to get yourself going again. She called to the hospital and said not to expect her. That was all right with them. There'd been a man brought in yesterday, but he'd died in the night. Nobody else now didn't have kin.

Except for stopping over to the convenience store for milk, Winnona stayed home all day. What she did puttering in the kitchen she could hardly remember, but it was what needed to be done.

Toward the end of the afternoon, Celladina stopped by, then Peaches. Winnona made fresh coffee. What Celladina wanted was for both of them to drive tomorrow to the rally with her in her van. Celladina was going to be taking out fried chicken and sandwiches and clothes they'd collected from the church.

"There'll be other girls bringing tables and chairs and blankets and coffee," Celladina explained. "They've got a couple of pickup trucks. All together, there'll be ten or twelve of us."

"Is Bobo coming?" Winnona asked.

"She might," Peaches cut in, "but she can't write about it for the paper. They're sending her to some land bank meetings — down at the county seat, I think. She has to go again tomorrow, but she said to me — I saw her at the store this morning — that she'll come on out tomorrow afternoon if she can get her sitter to pick up the boys at day care."

The phone rang and Winnona answered. Bobo was calling.

"You're going aren't you, Winnona?" she began quickly. "To the rally, I mean."

"Celladina and Peaches are here," Winnona told her.

"They're going." Up to that moment, Winnona hadn't wanted to let on she wasn't sure. She had a sore place in the back of one side of her throat. "I suppose there'll be a lot of crazy old wagons," she said.

"Wagons aren't the half of it," Bobo broke in. "There are children out there, Winnona, *infants*, whole families camping under trees in the rain and cooking on top of *stones*. There are feeble minded too — some of them with barely a stitch to put on and not even noticing."

"You've been there?"

"Just now but only for a few minutes because my sitter is sick and I had to take the boys with me. There were some Catholics there with doughnuts and coffee, but All Souls Day is coming up for them. It's something to do with Halloween, so they're busy tomorrow. It's the Protestants' turn. Those people need a real meal."

The thought of babies out when it was raining like last night made Winnona see things differently. Helpless people — not just old crows trailing around in rattletraps — were worth the effort.

Bobo wanted to speak to Celladina about picking up some of the boys' too small clothes she was going to leave on her side porch. While they talked, Winnona went to the icebox to get out the left over New England boiled dinner. It was almost five. Sam would be home soon.

Before she shut the door, the fullness of what was inside struck her — the milk in its plastic carton with a moist dribble down the side, the orange juice, the bread. She and Sam had seen hard times when they were kids, but they hadn't ever been without enough to eat.

Before the girls left, Winnona had promised to go. She wouldn't have to drive. She would ride in Celladina's van and bring a fresh-baked pumpkin pie.

After she and Sam had finished dinner, Winnona stayed in the kitchen to make pie, spilling out the oval pumpkin seeds in the sink. It was a big pumpkin. She decided to make two crusts.

When the pies were in the oven, Mary Lou called long distance from Cincinnati. She and her husband Dick were trying to decorate their new townhouse before the baby came. Dick, who was in insurance, had already done the living-dining room pale grey and the kitchen yellow. "Next weekend he's going to do our bedroom blue," Mary Lou was saying. "We're still deciding about the baby's room, but I think something neutral would be best — maybe cream — "

"You'd better hurry."

"I've got everything planned. If I nurse, I won't go back to the office for three or four months. If I don't, I could go back as soon as six weeks if the sitter's all right."

While Mary Lou was talking, Winnona noticed a pumpkin seed on the floor. She picked it up, placed it in her palm, and then set it in Sam's blue and white egg cup that was standing by the sink.

The seed, she mused while Mary Lou went on about room colors, could eventually father a whole field of pumpkins. The egg cup — hadn't it been part of the set that had come to her when Sam's mother's place was torn down for the interstate and his sister took almost everything but didn't want the old blue and white china?

She was beginning to smell the pies.

"What do you think, Mother?"

"Think?"

"About the color for the baby's room — "

Winnona didn't want to say pink, because she wasn't going to let on that she was hoping for a girl. For a grandchild, a girl would be more fun.

Trying to answer, she blurted out, " — milk — "

"You mean cream," Mary Lou corrected.

"That's what I was trying to say."

After Mary Lou hung up, Winnona took out the pies. They were done well, but not burnt. She cut a good slice from the extra one and then took it in to Sam, who was watching television.

He had his leg propped up, and she knew that meant it was hurting. He seldom mentioned the wounds. He got around fine. When it was raining though, or when he had to stand a long time in the damp like today pouring the floor, he felt it.

Winnona went back to the kitchen and got him a good big glass of milk. Then, after staring at the screen for a minute or so, she cleared away his plate and glass and headed upstairs. There were some things, she decided, and wounds were one of them, that didn't pass with time.

"You were dead to the world last night," Sam told her in the morning. "A couple more wagons went through — rattling loud enough to wake the dead. I got up to look, but you didn't even stir."

"I didn't hear them," she told him.

After Sam had gone, she remembered she had had a dream about Farmer Barker. It seemed he was driving the old milk wagon, and he wasn't sick at all. He looked fine.

Winnona was finishing her second cup of coffee when the phone rang. "Celladina can't drive," Peaches informed her. "She came down with the flu — same as Bobo's sitter. It's going around."

"What are we going to do?"

"We need the van because of all the things we've got to carry, but I don't drive stick shift — do you?"

"I can — " Winnona coughed. She had driven Sam's jeep

and even, long ago, tractors, but she'd been looking forward to not having to drive. She was still tired, there was something dragging her down. "Does Celladina mind?" she asked.

"No. You drive to her house and get the van. I'll meet you at the church in half an hour."

Later, after they had packed up everything and started off, Winnona found the old van harder to maneuver than she expected. Beyond the Murchison place where the ghost bags were still waving on the trees in a lonely way, the road had almost no shoulders. In some spots, sitting up so high in the van, you could see right down into the culvert with dark water in it. Passing the place where Sam was working she wanted to stop and ask him to take over, but of course, she didn't. She went on.

"It's a long time since I've been out this far," she told Celladina, gripping the wheel with both hands. The loaded van was heavy. It was a struggle to steer because the road was humped in the middle instead of graded.

"We used to come here when we were in school," Peaches said.

"There were picnics — "

"But now they all go to the new beach nearer to town."

The road had turned to dirt and sand. You could smell the river, but you couldn't see it. There were tall pines on either side.

"Look out — " Peaches warned.

Catching sight of the turn to the left, Winnona saw she had angled in toward the meeting place too sharply. One side of the van was deep in a wagon rut — they were tipping —

Peaches screamed. Winnona twisted the wheels to the right and gave it the gas. Like a bucking horse, the van leaped forward, and then, before she could brake it, careened across the

furrows of an old field quite a ways before it stopped beside
three or four rusty bicycles piled in a heap — and stalled.

"Whew — " Winnona just sat there. Finally, she took her
hands off the wheel.

"Are we gonna get out?" Peaches said finally.

"I guess." She looked around. Not far off, nearer to the
river, people had parked every which way — cars, trucks, wagons, motorcycles, everything. "No point in going further."

Peaches opened her door. Winnona opened hers. They
both got out. Winnona walked around to the back of the van
and stood there. She was weak in the legs.

She had almost forgotten the place, it had been so long.
The land sloped up to the north like a table with one leg
shorter. The high part of the enormous open field was way up
to the left where you could see down to the water from the
tall, sandy banks. Beyond there, way away, One Mile Hill
heaved up at the horizon and the trees began.

"Where is everybody?" Peaches asked.

Winnona pointed to the place at the top of the banks —
the old picnic spot. There, so far away they were no more
than dark figures against the pale sky, the people were gathered.

"We can't carry the chicken and sandwiches all that way,"
Peaches said.

"The other girls have pickup trucks," Winnona reminded
her. "When they get here, we'll pack everything in with them
and take it up. That van isn't mine. I don't want to try it."

"It could be a while before they get here. They had so
many girls to stop for . . What'll we do now?"

"Go up, I guess. See what's going on."

They began the climb in silence. Peaches led the way.

At the top, when they got there, it was pretty much what
Bobo had said. There were families with children — probably

staying under the big trees overlooking the river where sheets were hanging up. There were people, too, who didn't look as if they knew their own names. One, a girl who had to be six months gone, didn't seem to have anything on but a man's tan raincoat drawn around her and a pair of old white sneakers cut out at the toes. The half-grown boy beside her — blank-faced and with maybe even less sense — was wearing a woman's ruffled skirt and a blanket wrapped around him like an Indian.

There were wagons that had been drawn all the way up, and the reason, Winnona suspected, was that people slept under them when it rained. There were horses and mules grazing around behind them. Leaving Peaches talking to a tired-looking woman with a little baby, Winnona poked around and found the wagon that had come by the house. It was empty, and there was no one near it except the piebald, standing with his head raised as if sniffing the wind. After a minute, she spotted what looked like the bundles the wagon had been carrying dumped out under some bushes.

Coming close, she saw that what was in the dirty sacks was trash, just as she'd thought. For spilling out from the splitting burlap were dirty rags, rusty cans, half burned coal lumps, battered bricks and dried corn ears with the kernels bitten away. Nothing useful, nothing to wear or eat — or even read, because the newspapers that were tangled with the rest of the mess were so rumpled, so yellowed, they would have fallen apart in your hands. What was the point, then, of hauling it all up here? There was no explanation. The driver, of course, was nowhere to be seen.

Winnona went back to where Peaches was. The woman, she learned, had to wash the diapers in the river and hope they'd dry on some bush. The baby had thrush. The husband had been blinded in an accident at work. He was back under the trees, waiting. There wasn't anything to do but lead him around by his hand.

Bobo had been right, Winnona saw, but it was worse than she'd said. What Bobo hadn't said though was that there was more to it. It wasn't just a gathering — it was like a camp meeting.

For, coming from a little higher up, she heard people humming a hymn. The people standing here, she realized, were waiting for a service or a sermon or something like it. Then, turning toward the river, she saw there was someone standing way up on a rock, at the edge of the flat place where the picnic tables used to be. That was where the hymn was coming from. Peaches was going there, and so were all the others. Peaches had the baby because the woman had gone to get her blind husband. Winnona followed along. "Land. . ." intoned the voice of the preacher, "when we get back our land . . . ."

Without being told, Winnona knew who the preacher was. Standing up on the rock, he looked even leaner, taller and older than he had driving the wagon The wind was worrying his long black coat with the rusty sheen, winding and unwinding the folds around his stovepipe legs. His hair — she would have known that yellow white hay mop anywhere — was whipping back and forth across his face and into his watery eyes.

"Winnona — " Peaches pulled at her sleeve, "the girls are here."

Yes, looking way down to the bottom of the hill, Winnona saw two pickups parked not far from Celladina's van. "What'll we do?"

"You stay here," Peaches directed, "you look worn out. I'll go down and help them get the stuff out of the van and into the trucks. Give me the keys."

Winnona passed them over.

"And here — " Peaches plopped the small, sleeping baby

into Winnona's arms.

After she had gone, Winnona realized that she didn't even know whether the poor wisp of a blotchy-faced thing in the dirty white blanket was a boy or a girl. Half way down the hill, she noticed, was a man in a wheel chair, was struggling over the furrows. How he had gotten even that far and where he had come from, Winnona couldn't imagine. She wanted to find someone to help, but then she saw that four big fellows — farm boys from the look of them — had come along behind and lifted the wheel chair right up. It wasn't but a minute till they bore him by on their shoulders like somebody in a procession. The cripple was a veteran with both legs missing, Winnona saw. He was wearing an old army shirt and cap, and there was an American flag attached to one of his chair handles, sticking up high.

There was no point standing still. Winnona followed the others, carrying the baby and stepping carefully so she wouldn't stumble. As she climbed through the stubble, rusty-colored crickets rose in front of her, jumping to either side.

"The sowers of the seed," the black-suited spectre on the stone was saying in a singsong way, "have got the right — " he paused, "to — REAP."

The baby's eyes opened. A little hand slid out of the blanket. The tiny palm was wrinkled; it looked old.

"The harvest — " the old crow cawed, "the land. . .is OURS."

What did that mean? What land? What harvest? This was a group, for the most part, that wasn't going to get anything but tares. They were all hungry, pure and simple. She was hungry herself, even though she'd had a good breakfast. The baby, a bubble forming over its little white lips, was crying softly. It was probably hungry too.

Winnona felt angry. Everything was turned around. What

right did that crazy have to bring folks out when there was
nothing here for them? She felt like taking the hungry baby up
to the stone and throwing it at him. Why, in a country like
this, wasn't there enough for everyone? Enough land, enough
food, enough jobs?

Why wasn't there a place these people belonged? Why
wasn't there somebody that cared? Why was everything, she
wondered, letting the baby suck her finger, discombobulated?
She thought of Farmer Barker dying miles away from his
daughter in the hospital. She thought of the all-alone girl in
the field who would be having that baby — who knows where.

"Green fields," the preacher bellowed, still running off at
the mouth, "fruitful valleys . . . ."

Looking around, Winnona saw the girls were on their way.
The two pickups were bumping slowly up the hill. She was
glad. Then the mother of the baby came back with her husband behind, holding her shoulder. He was a good-looking fellow even with his eyes shut — but ragged. When the mother
took the baby back to nurse it under her blouse, Winnona was
very glad.

The relief, she realized, was partly because she was cold at
the bottom of her stomach. Or maybe it was that she had to
go to the bathroom. She wasn't sure. To be safe, she headed
away from the others towards where the wagons were. There,
standing on the far side of the terrible old black cart, she
decided she was going to be sick. Except, when she leaned
over, she could only cough a little, and afterwards, spit to clear
her throat.

What happened next she was never sure of afterwards, but
somehow, the wagon began to move. Maybe it was because of
one of the horses grazing just beyond, maybe the wheels hadn't
been locked or blocked with broken bricks, but it seemed to
Winnona that it was the preacher's screaming that had

unloosed everything, set what wasn't supposed to move in motion.

Whatever it was, the cart, after rolling grandly and somberly past Winnona, gained speed. The hill was steep, there was nothing to hold it. For an instant, Winnona was afraid the pickups might be in the way of it, but no, the girls had got to the top. Then, turning around, Winnona saw that the horses were coming.

If the cart had still been there, she could have gotten behind it — or under it. But there was nothing near except an old red rig that was open like the ribs of a skeleton. It was too late anyway — a woman was screaming, people were running.

The last thing Winnona remembered was the piebald coming towards her like Armageddon with three mules behind him. Their hooves shook the earth like trumpets, and the piebald was as huge as an apparition come down from the sky — flying like Pegasus. He was above her, she was staring at his enormous muzzle head on. She saw his eyes' redness, smelled his nostrils' smoke, felt his hooves' weight. . . .

She had had the flu, that was the first thing someone told her later that made sense. She had been knocked down by the horses — but only bruised, nothing broken. The someone was Sam; he was sitting beside her bed in the hospital. She had had the bad kind of flu — worse than what Celladina and the woman who worked for Bobo had had. For a while, it had been touch and go.

Sam had been coming every day. He had good news for her. She was a grandmother. Sam had a picture of the baby, which had come early. He also showed her a picture of his house he was building. It was almost framed in.

Later, when Winnona was home again, she and Peaches pieced things together as best they could. The cart had gotten loose, the horses had stampeded. By the time the ladies got to her she was out cold, so, leaving the coffee and the sandwiches and everything else up there, they had taken her in one of the pickups to the hospital. Later that same day, they got Bobo and went out there again, and Bobo drove Celladina's van home. By then, there was almost nobody there.

"Nobody?" Winnona asked.

"Not many. I guess they got scared because of the horses acting up and somebody being hurt. Bobo put something about it in the paper later. It got more play than Halloween."

"But where did they all go?"

"Scattered to the four winds, I guess. No, that's not true, there were some sick enough themselves to go to the hospital. One girl had a baby, I heard. Some got taken to the homeless shelter up at the county seat. A couple of boys got taken on farms as hired hands. Where the rest went, I never heard."

"Oh." Winnona asked no more questions, but if someone had questioned her (they didn't) she would have told a different story. What she remembered — plain as the hand before her face — was that after the rally she'd gone back to somebody's old farm, maybe Mr. Barker's. After that, she'd stopped by Sam's cellar where the preacher and his wagon were laid out on the new cement — neat and clean. The piebald, though, wasn't there. He had cantered sky-high to the blue moon, and nobody could get him back.

When you remembered things like that, Winnona reflected, it was best not to dwell on them. She stayed weak for a while, but she and Sam made it out to Cincinnati for Christmas. The baby was actually four weeks ahead of time. Mary Lou, who was always so good at numbers, had counted wrong. Anyway, the baby's room was painted pink, and

Winnona was glad.

It wasn't until the worst of the winter was over that Winnona felt ready to visit at the hospital again. Finally though, she called and said she'd come.

The next Monday, a sunny morning when the snow was nearly melted, Winnona went over. In the little garden beside the hospital parking lot, someone had put an ironclad wagon wheel in the center of the bed. There, poking through the grey snow between the spokes, were some little white flowers.

Winnona wouldn't have been ashamed to say she was getting too old to like surprises. Of course, she wasn't expecting one when the nurse took her down the hall to a room across from where Farmer Barker had been. Inside, the old man who was dying was lying quietly with his face turned away toward the window. Winnona, though, would have recognized the yellow-white straw hair anywhere.

Catching her breath, Winnona stopped dead.

"I told him about you," the nurse said. "He hasn't got folks. He's been waiting for you."

Winnona got herself in hand. Professionally, with hardly a hesitation, she went to the corner and got a folding chair. "I guess," she told the nurse before she sat down, "you might say I've been waiting for him."

Copies of *Horse & Cart* can be ordered from:
The Wineberry Press
3207 Macomb Street NW
Washington, D.C. 20008

PHOTO BY: *LAURA SCHLEUSSNER*

Born in Rome, N.Y., Elisabeth Stevens grew up in Maplewood, N.J., and graduated from Columbia High School. She received a B.A. from Wellesley College and a M.A. with High Honors in Contemporary Literature from Columbia University.

As a journalist, Ms. Stevens was the art critic and a reporter for *The Washington Post* (1965-66), the editorial page art critic for *The Wall Street Journal* (1969-1972), and the art critic for *The Trenton Times* (1974-77). From 1978-86, she was the art and architecture critic for *The Baltimore Sun.*

Her criticism, fiction and poetry also appear in many other newspapers, magazines, and journals: *The New York Times, The Philadelphia Inquirer, Life, Mademoiselle, The Atlantic, The New Republic, McCall's, Bookworld, House & Garden, Réalités, Museum News, Art News, Artforum, Art in America, Playgirl, Confrontation, Chariton Review, Wind Magazine, Belles Lettres, Portland Review, Louisville Review, Late Knocking, Maryland Poetry Review, Women's Review of Books, New Renaissance, Kirkus Review.*

Ms. Stevens won a National Endowment for the Arts Art Critic's Fellowship, as well as the A.D. Emmart Memorial Award for Maryland journalists and a citation for critical writing from The Baltimore Washington Newspaper Guild, AFL-CIO. She was awarded a Maryland State Arts Council literary works-in-progress grant for poetry and a Baltimore Mayor's Committee on Art & Culture (MACAC) creative development grant for the illustrations of this volume of stories. She has been a fellow at The MacDowell Colony, The Virginia Center for the Creative Arts, and The Ragdale Foundation.

Elisabeth Stevens' Guide to Baltimore's Inner Harbor, an architecturally oriented introduction to Baltimore's Renaissance, was published in 1981 by Stemmer House. Her subsequent books include: *Fire & Water: Six Stories*, Perivale Press, 1983, and *Children of Dust: Portraits & Preludes*, New Poets Series, 1985.

A widow, Ms. Stevens is the mother of a daughter who is a Classicist. They live in Baltimore.

Other works from The Wineberry Press:

GET WITH IT, LORD by Beatrice M. Murphy

SWIMMING OUT OF THE COLLECTIVE UNCONSCIOUS
   by Maxine Combs

NO ONE IS LISTENING by Elizabeth Follin-Jones

20 / 20 VISIONARY ECLIPSE & THE WHORLING
   TRY/ANGLES by Judith McCombs

FINDING THE NAME, an anthology
   edited by Elisavietta Ritchie